MIKE
CHAMP

MIKE CHAMP

TIMOTHY A. SUCHLA

TATE PUBLISHING
AND ENTERPRISES, LLC

Published by Tate Publishing & Enterprises, LLC
127 E. Trade Center Terrace | Mustang, Oklahoma 73064 USA
1.888.361.9473 | www.tatepublishing.com

Tate Publishing is committed to excellence in the publishing industry. The company reflects the philosophy established by the founders, based on Psalm 68:11,
"The Lord gave the word and great was the company of those who published it."

Book design copyright © 2013 by Tate Publishing, LLC. All rights reserved.
Cover design by Jan Sunday Quilaquil
Interior design by Jomar Ouano

Published in the United States of America
ISBN: 978-1-62854-854-9
1. Fiction / Sports
2. Fiction / Christian / General
13.10.17

DEDICATION

This book is dedicated to all my children who I love with all my heart and to my wife Rachel who said she believed in me. I've been diligent in my hard work in hopes of leaving part of myself behind for all of you, so you may get a glimpse of who I am and what I stand for in the pages I have written here. I'm so sorry I was not around more for you, especially during the times children need their daddy the most. I'm sorry, Katie; a child should never have to see their father's mistakes while at the lowest point of his life. God bless my children.

CHAPTER 1

"There are two outs in the bottom of the ninth," roared the announcer as dad and I huddled around the transistor radio straining to hear. We enjoyed listening to the colorful calls of a familiar voice, along with nostalgic stories of players past and present even while attending the games. The crowd turned deafening, the air was electric, and we all believed Champ was going to get it done, like he always had. This would be Champ's second World Series MVP in the last five years. Dad and I knew all his stats being our favorite player. Between the ages of five and twelve, I had seen him pitch many times, but this time I would forever hold closest to my heart, being the last for me and my dad together. The umpire threw his fist in the air for a strike three. Champ tossed his cap skyward, fell to his knees, and buried his face in his glove, possibly to cover his joyous tears. The team ran to the center of the diamond, hoisted their pitcher up on their shoulders and carried him around the field. Never had I seen such excitement in the crowd and on the players' faces. The entire stadium chanted his name in unison with the intensity and precision of a marching band. Everyone knew if it was not for his gritty, determined heroics this victory would not have been accomplished.

My dad looked down at me amidst all the celebration and with a gleam in his eye said, "Well champ, what should we do to celebrate?"

Over the years, this memory played in my mind many times, but this time it didn't bring back the usual warmth but rather a chilling feel. "In the hospital," I said out loud transitioning back to reality, "did I hear that correctly?" These twenty-five-year-old flashbacks were more frequent lately, and the only reason I could think to attribute the blame was stress. I had been walking down the sidewalk in my daydream stupor, and now found myself standing in front of an old rickety house with two elderly gentlemen sitting on the front porch next to a heater listening to the radio.

One of the men shook his head in response to me, "Yes sir, we heard it too, they say there's something wrong with him but they didn't say what." It was late morning, cold and windy, but hearing that piece of news hurt more than the stinging on my frozen ears. The hospital mentioned was conveniently close. I took a moment to contemplate the situation, then another to calculate putting myself into it.

"What the hell, what's the worst thing that can happen?" I worked on convincing myself even more out loud so as to not allow wimping out of the idea ricocheting around in my head. With a crazy daring mood persuading me along, I took the challenge of investigating to see if there was anything I could do for the old ballplayer, and with nothing to lose for trying, off I went.

I quickened my steps as I approached the hospital with a strange nagging urgency pushing me along. I didn't know why, I didn't know what I would do or say, but something would come to me, it always did. I had a way of finagling through things being a good communicator; some have even gone so far as to call me a slick talker. My whole life I've been told I was a 'little off' anyway and doing things others wouldn't or didn't understand was my way of making life a little more entertaining.

Chaos only began to describe the scene entering the hospital lobby with people going every which way in a fast paced hustle and bustle. A nice young woman at the information desk helped by telling me what floor Champ was on. I pondered while continuing on my way if her quick service was due to niceness or the desire to resume texting. I zipped down the hall and into the elevator with two young nurses entering behind me.

"Fifth floor," one asked if I'd push the button while the other continued her talking without interruption. The little talker looked no more than five feet tall and a hundred pounds, white, very cute, with long brown hair and couldn't be more than one year removed from nursing school. The listener—very intent on hearing every word, nodding frequently—was a larger black female, delightful in appearance herself and probably a couple years her senior.

"Ah-hum," I cleared my throat. "Do you ladies work on the fifth floor? I just found out my father checked in so I rushed over," knowing Mike was about the right age to be my dad. I hoped my shifty impropriety wouldn't cause any harm, but I also knew the room number of someone famous might not be so easy to come by.

"Yes, we do work on the fifth floor, we're getting ready to start our shift," said the listener. "My name is Trish and this little midget is my sidekick, we call her Jen. We'll find out what room your dad's in when we get to the nurse's station, what's your dad's name?"

"Mike...Mike Champ is his name."

The door opened and the two nurses quickly scurried off as if cutting it very close to their starting time. I decided to go in the other direction and moseyed down the hallway acting somewhat like I knew where I was going, glancing nonchalantly into each room I passed. At the end of the hall, I could see straight into the room where Mr. Champ was being helped into a wheelchair by an orderly. His appearance was nearly the same to me but without the baseball uniform and more fragile. It had been many years since I'd seen him—and even then he was on the pitcher's mound and I was in the stands with my dad, usually behind home plate— although I had seen him up close once shortly after he retired at an autograph signing. I remember clearly the giant brown mustache and the words "what can I do for you little cowboy?" when I held up my baseball card to be signed. Mike was a very large man about six feet four inches tall with broad shoulders. He towered above my father when they shook hands, and he gave my dad a wink and a slap on the back. Even at twelve, I could tell he appreciated the attention of the adoring fans, especially the kids. He seemed to have a special place in his heart for baseball and for those who loved the game as well.

"Hello," I said poking my head in the door. "Trish and Jen said I could go ahead and take him wherever he needs to be," I stated confidently pretending I had a clue as I tried to pull off the innocent stunt, still reassuring myself no harm would come from weaseling my way into help.

"Oh, okay, if that's what they told ya. I'll let you take him right on down to the lab. I guess they're wanting to poke him with some needles," the man chuckled as he put the finishing touches on situating Mr. Champ. The man played the part well with his uniform, as if an orderly stepped right out of a movie. He was an older gentleman but seemingly in good physical condition, tall, slender, very clean cut with a well groomed mustache and hair. You could've easily stuck a cowboy hat and boots on him and called him sheriff in an old western with his combination of drawl and distinguished demeanor. When he looked in my direction, I saw why he might not have chosen sheriff as a career path; I couldn't tell if his direct attention was at me or the clock on the wall. Slightly uncomfortable, I simply smiled back at him and tried not to focus my attention on his wandering eye. He smiled back at me with an uncommon exceedingly warm expression—the old rare kind I only remember seeing as a child during a time when people still meant what they said.

After a few moments of soaking up the man's pleasant sunshine, I broke the awkward silence and rattled out, "You betcha I'm sure he can't wait for those needles."

"Well," he said, "my name is Henry, I'll probably be seeing you around." Henry walked to the door as I walked toward Mike. He turned in the doorway and said, "You behave now." Mike and I faced one another a little confused, and I glanced back at the doorway with the obvious question but he was gone.

Without Henry, I directed the question to my new patient, "Who was he talking to?"

Mike turned up to me, "I'm pretty sure he was talking to you, you look like a troublemaker."

"Thanks a lot Mr. Champ but I could tell by the angle of his head, that comment was definitely directed at you," I shot back standing my ground.

"Maybe," Mike started with a stern look, "he was talking to both of us, and who the hell are you anyway?"

"Oh I'm sorry, let me introduce myself. My name is Tim Smith and I'm here to take you to the lab."

"Do you work for the hospital? You don't have a uniform on."

"Well, not exactly," I replied slowly thinking of my next move.

"What does not exactly mean?" His eyes stayed fixed on me allowing for no escape.

"Well, let's just say I'm here to be helpful and supportive, what's wrong with you anyway?"

"I'm not sure yet. They're going to do some tests today and hopefully find out and you changed the subject."

"Do you remember the final game of the last World Series you pitched in Mr. Champ?"

"Yes, of course I remember, I was there," he replied with a touch of sarcasm.

"I was there too, with my dad who passed away shortly after, it's one of the best memories of my entire life. When I heard on the radio you were here, I was prompted to come and see if there was anything I could do to help. Besides, the hospital has many volunteers you know. Where's your family anyway? Do you have children? Are you married?" I tried question bombardment to redirect his attention away from my role at the hospital.

Mike lowered his eyes to the ground. "I have no wife and I haven't talked to my son in years, if it's any of your business."

"Well then since you don't have a line of people at the door begging to push your wheelchair around, I suggest you not complain and let's get you down to the lab."

Mike grabbed the wheels so the chair wouldn't roll. "I'll let you take me to the lab on one condition."

"And what's that?" I inquired calmly camouflaging my nervousness while repeatedly pleading silently *please, please, please*, in my head. I wasn't sure what he was about to say, but I really wanted to hang out with my childhood hero.

"We need to swing by the cafeteria on the way, I'm starving."

"That's all you want?" I waited for his head to nod. I learned years ago selling vacuum cleaners getting a sale required a series of commitments. "Let's shake on it then," I added, extending my hand to seal the deal.

"How about you just start pushing me kid?"

Kid, made me feel good being in my midthirties. I jumped behind, hiding a ridiculously happy face. "That sounds great Mr. Champ," I declared as we set out. "It's the hospital cafeteria or bust for us."

I rolled him down the hallway, purposely avoiding the nurse's station, and commented along the stroll that I was surprised at the lack of media here trying to get a story about the baseball legend. "I told them when I filled out the paperwork downstairs and was admitted earlier I didn't want to talk to any reporters." His response came across gruff and I couldn't tell if it was due to his sickness, worry, or if life had backed over him too many times causing him to be miserable. Throughout my life, I had taken notice that people who have experienced a lot of unhappiness in their lives tend to get grumpier as they age, and he already disclosed a sad fact when mentioning his son.

I felt bad for the old-timer and attempted to lighten the mood. "This is a fine wheelchair you have sir, I'll be your chauffeur for the rest of the day, please keep your arms and legs in at all times." My jokes bounced off Mike's grimace and by the worn and weak look of him, my best guess concluded he mostly was not feeling real well. Selfishly though, I was glad to be here with him but obviously under different circumstances would have been better. After our elevator ride to the first floor, getting directions twice, and fifteen minutes of roaming the halls, we finally found the cafeteria. There were several places under construction along the way and poor placement of detour signs hadn't helped. I may have also fiddle-farted a bit, chattering away not wanting the time with him to end too soon.

"Well, here you go Mr. Champ sir, one hospital cafeteria for your fine dining pleasure." Even though Mike wasn't laughing or even smiling at my aspiring humor, I felt confident he was enjoying my company. My intuition told me he didn't want to be alone and I trusted my gut on these matters being very perceptive. I was sure this is where I needed to be right now.

"Mr. Champ?"

"Call me Mike."

"Okay Mike, I'm guessing you don't have any money to buy food. I mean I can see part of your butt from my vantage point, so I'm quite confident you don't have a wallet hidden anywhere back here, nor do you have any front pockets in your fancy hospital gown."

"Oh crap," Mike blurted, "I forgot about money."

"That's all right Mr. Champ, I got you covered. Get whatever you want, but...," the light turned on in the sneaky part of my brain. "You could do me a small favor later," my cheeks swelled up to a childlike innocent smile with my hands gesturing that it was no big deal.

"Oh really, and what kind of favor would that be?"

"Well," my mind scrambled for proper word selection to gently ease into full disclosure of my slight truth infraction. "I would appreciate it if you didn't get too upset with something, I kind of, accidentally told the nurses." I was getting a little embarrassed and didn't want to blow the opportunity of befriending Mike.

"And what did you accidentally tell the nurses?" He turned his full attention from food gathering to me with a raised eyebrow glare.

"I'm sure you'll find out anyway. I was hoping you wouldn't take it too seriously, heck you may even think it's funny."

My stalling had stalled out, and I needed to come clean with the truth. As I opened my mouth to confess, Mike lowered his eyebrows and turned back to his donut decision. "Should I go maple bar or glazed?" Before I could respond he followed up with, "Don't worry kid, I'm too old to get mad and I realized years ago as a young ballplayer, the word fan is short for fanatic. From what I've seen of you so far, I'm sure it will be interesting." At this point, I could see Mike was more engaged in the menu than whatever I told the nurses, so I decided to go back to my role as supportive hospital volunteer and gently work my way into the beginning of phase one pre-friend.

"Do you think you have enough stuff on your tray?" Mike grabbed what appeared to be the final piece of his food pile pyramid; a creation that would have made the ancient Egyptians proud and included two sandwiches, a bag of chips, one donut, a yogurt, and an apple. I rolled him over and parked the wheelchair at a table and added for good measure, "are you sure you didn't forget anything?"

"Oh yeah, thanks for asking, can you grab me a soda?" With that comment and with no help from my jokes, he finally surrendered a grin rivaling that of the Grinch that stole Christmas.

"I guess you think that's pretty funny?" I commented over my shoulder walking back toward the drinks.

"And could you grab me a milk too? Make it 2 percent!" he yelled back. After waiting in line several more minutes and only a few steps from delivering the goods, I saw her. Approaching like a locomotive with a full head of steam, Trish, the nice nurse I met earlier in the elevator and she did not appear too happy.

"Where have you two been? You were supposed to be at the lab twenty minutes ago. I would have delivered you there myself Mr. Champ, but you told nurse Holts you preferred and were up to the task of taking yourself down."

"You see—" I started but was abruptly interrupted.

"You're not being a very good son, not getting your dad directly where he needs to be." There it was, out in the open. She let the cat out of the bag before I had a chance and I cringed as I turned my attention over to Mike.

"Well, young nurse lady," Mike jumped in looking up at me with yet another sinister grin now knowing my dilemma. "My son's a little slow if you know what I mean. I told him we didn't have time to stop and eat, but he wouldn't listen. I am of course too weak to argue with him." He put his two hands to his chest as if auditioning for the school play. "I believe it started when he was about three, his dear mother accidentally slammed his head in the car door. The poor lad has been equal to the stupid side of a donkey ever since." He not only caught my indiscretion but was running away with it on his way to accept an Academy Award.

"Well, I don't care," snapped the not-very-nice-anymore nurse Trish. "You better pull your head out and get your two little butts down to the lab, and I mean now. You're going to have me in so much hot water I'll be turning red, and that color doesn't suit me. And you certainly don't need all this junk food in your condition." She grabbed a sandwich, chips, and the donut off Mike's tray, then the soda out of my hand and sped off back down the hallway stuffing the donut in her mouth on the way.

Mike looked up at me with a not-so-well-hidden pout. "Did she just swipe my food?" I nodded. "Son, huh?" He could see my discomfort but didn't seem to mind my little white lie. "Let's go chauffeur, but you're buying me more food later."

"Yes, Dad."

CHAPTER 2

After our trip to the lab and an array of tests involving a few different floors of the hospital, our final stop was in a room where Mike was attached to several monitors by multiple sets and series of color-coded wires—an ensemble that could potentially cause even a journeyman electrician a migraine. I could clearly see the steady accumulation of exhaustion and worry on Mike's face as we were shuttled around throughout the day and without him saying anything, I rendered myself under the impression he knew something terrible was wrong but wanted confirmation and specifics from the doctors. We were now alone in the room. Our joking had come to an end, and I tried to fill the space with positive comments while we anxiously waited for some answers.

"You know Mike, they can fix just about anything these days with all the new medical technology. I'm sure everything will be fine," I attempted to express my logic with all the upbeat enthusiasm I could muster.

"You know Tim, I understand if you need to be somewhere else. I'm sure the novelty of hanging around an old baseball player has worn off by now and I'll be fine." I knew he was trying to give me an out, knowing this would be extremely difficult for anyone, whether they were close to the sickly person or not and more so if they really didn't want to be around.

I responded accordingly, "Nope, I don't need to be anywhere. I'd rather not leave if that's all right with you, except maybe to slip down to the cafeteria and rustle up some grub; they're not very good about feeding you around here." Mike perked up with the mention of food while simultaneously the young Dr. Jim entered the room with a paper-filled clipboard in hand. We called him the young Dr. Jim because he looked under thirty, and we heard his mother call him on more than one occasion during the day.

"Yes mom, no mom, of course I will mom, mom I really need to go, I am a doctor you know," so on and so forth. Of course earlier, Mike had to let him know that he had hairs in his mustache older than the young doctor too. Despite being young, short, and boyishly cute (according to the nurses), he exuded tremendous confidence and ability. Much of the staff had commented that despite his age, he had a brilliant medical mind, and we were in good hands under his care. The young doctor walked over and sat on the edge of Mike's bed opposite to where I was sitting in a large cushion chair with armrests.

"Mr. Champ, I should explain the various details of your tests and maybe a few things about these different charts along with the numbers in your blood work." He paused with an uncomfortable deep breath. "But I won't, I'll just get right to the point. The simple prognosis is," he stopped again, took his glasses off and did the typical upper nose pinch and rub you see people do with glasses when that spot between their eyes gets sore. He then turned down toward the floor away from Mike and my view, and I knew something was wrong when he continued looking away.

"Are you okay, Doc?" Mike said in a gentle voice leaning forward patting him on the shoulder.

"I'm sorry," he turned back around, now with a hanky in his hand wiping his eyes and before I had time to think how strange that was, he started again. "Mr. Champ, it boils down to this, your heart is sick, it's old and tired and is probably going to quit on you very soon. I can't say when for sure and there is no cure. The only thing we can do is put you on some medication that may help give you more time, add you to a waiting list for a transplant, and hope for the best. I am truly sorry I wish I had better news." His words induced an instant lump in my throat and tightening of my stomach. I couldn't believe what I heard while still noticing the extreme difficulty the young doctor had in delivering the news as the words stumbled from his mouth, but he said what needed to be said and I admired him for that.

The doctor partially pulled himself together and we both concentrated on Mike, waiting for a reaction and after several moments he calmly replied. "Well, that's all right Doc. It's not your fault." He then shot a wink at me, turned back to the young doctor and said, "Say, aren't I supposed to be the one red faced?" acknowledging the distraught young man.

Dr. Jim met Mike's comment with a partial smile, blew his nose in the hanky, and started an explanation. "I apologize for not being more professional Mr. Champ, I haven't gotten used to delivering bad news to people, not to mention you're an icon in my family. I still hear Paul Bunyan-type stories about you on the pitcher's mound dueling with the very best every time my dad and uncles get together for the holidays. It was the good old days according to them, when there were good jobs to go around and everyone took pride in the baseball team and the city. My dad, now a retired dockworker, sometimes watches old games all day when he sits in his easy chair while reminiscing and complaining about how the world has changed. He's a strong, proud man and when I look at him close during these times, I can see a sad longing for the way things used to be and knowing they'll never return. I think it's his way of grudgingly accepting the loss of his youth."

Mike had been leaning back slightly in his bed and now sat straight up and put his big arms around the young doctor who was still struggling with his emotions. "How about I'll sign a baseball for your dad."

"Thank you Mr. Champ, my dad would love that."
I was in complete awe, never in my life had I seen such
a divine gesture from a man who was just told… he was
very near his end. Mike instantly transformed himself
from my childhood hero to a giant man that I now
wanted to emulate.

The young doctor stood up. "We'd like to keep you
around here for a while to keep an eye on you if that
would be all right?"

"Sure Doc, whatever you say."

Dr. Jim turned to me and said, "Can I talk to you
for a minute in the hallway?" I gave Mike a pat on the
shoulder as I got up letting him know I'd be right back.

In the hall, Dr. Jim spoke in a low solemn voice
as if we were already at Mike's funeral and he wanted
to lean across the aisle and tell me something during
the eulogy. "Since you're his only family here, I need to
make sure you fully understand there's a good chance
he doesn't have a lot of time. Other family members
that may want to see him before he goes should
not dillydally."

"Of course," I nodded in numb disbelief.

The young doctor started to walk away, spun
around, and spoke again but with renewed contrition
like he somehow caused Mike's condition. "The world
will not be a better place without your dad, I'm so sorry,"
then turned and left me standing alone in the hallway.

The hospital that I once thought of as a gateway
for new life entering the world and a place of healing
the sick and afflicted now stood in my mind as a giant

monument of suffering and death. A wave of shock pounded me as I realized what started out to be an innocent white lie to possibly meet and help my boyhood idol had now turned into an awesome responsibility. My neck went limp, my chin hit my chest, and with my eyes closed I whispered inwardly, "What have I done?" I took a moment, a few deep breaths to try and regain my composure. I needed to be cool for Mike's sake, I just had no idea what to say. I used my sleeve to wipe sweat from my brow, inhaled one more large calming breath and opened the door to go back in. I stopped in the doorway for an instant seeing him alone in bed, and I knew it had to be a good thing with me being here, regardless of how I came to be in this position because he had no one else right now. "Hey Mike," I said softly. "Is there anyone I can call for you, brothers, sisters, parents, anyone at all?"

"No, there is no one," Mike grumbled. "I grew up in several different foster homes. I have no family except for...well, no one."

"But didn't you say you had a son?"

"We haven't spoken in twenty years Tim, and besides none of this is your responsibility." I felt a little hurt with that comment but once again I could tell he was only trying to let me off the hook, and I wasn't having it.

"You know it is now Mike, and I'll be damned if I'm going anywhere and leaving you here by yourself." I was following my instincts again and by the expressive cast of relief on his face, I knew my bold reply was the correct response. Mike wasn't the type to ask for help, and now more than ever, he didn't want to be alone. "Now then are you hungry? You haven't eaten in a while. Do you want something to drink, a soda maybe?"

"No, I'm fine, would you sit a minute and relax." The prior gruffness in his voice had dissipated to a troubled tranquil, and he lay back on his bed and closed his eyes.

After a few minutes of silence, three nurses entered the room—Trish, Jen, and an older nurse I hadn't seen before. The unknown nurse was tall and thin, with a pretty yet stern face. I estimated her age to be about forty-five. She made direct eye contact with us and said, "My name is nurse Holts, you'll be mostly seeing us while you are here. The three of us cover this floor from 10:00 a.m. to 10:00 p.m., almost every day since we're short of nurses at this hospital. We're here to take the very best care of you and keep you comfortable as possible during your time here. Do you have any questions?" She finished speaking and glanced to her right at the younger two nurses and them noticing this made an effort to stand up straighter as if they could feel her eyes telling them not to slouch.

"No," Mike said, "I'm fine."

"He could use another blanket."

Nurse Holts glanced to her right again and nurse Jen sped off, "Yes ma'am."

"It looks like he's ready for his dinner now."

One last time at nurse Trish and she was off, "Yes ma'am."

Mike and I made wide-eyed contact with a mirrored expression of uneasiness, and I lip-synched the word "wow" to Mike then lead myself into nervously thinking I would be sent off to errand next. To say nurse Holts ran a tight ship may have been selling her leadership skills short, I theorized she may have acquired her executive abilities in the military. "Okay then, if you're all right for now, I'll be going, and I'll have her bring in an extra dinner for you," pointing at me.

"Thank you," I respectfully replied.

Shortly after nurse Holts left, the speedy little nurse Jen reentered the room with a couple of blankets. "Okay, here you guys go and she'll be in with your dinner in a minute."

"Was that the boss?" I asked, but with some reservation hitched to the question. Jen was quick to pick up on my meaning by the hesitation in my voice, and it was possible others may have ventured into this subject area before making it a familiar territory for her.

"Oh no, nurse Holts is great, she just seems to have a rough and tough exterior, inside she's like a teddy bear. Her demeanor has always been that of a serious person but recently," her voice got quieter as she cautiously glanced over her shoulder at the door. "I think it's her broken heart that makes her appear more that way." She had our full attention and we leaned into a small huddle around Mike's bed as Jen continued talking in a hushed whisper. "Her husband was a doctor and was killed six months ago in the war. Even though she never misses work and sometimes smiles a little, we all know something inside her died with him. She's been like a second mother to Trish and I, and we both know she would do anything for us, we're very lucky to be learning from her. She's the most respected nurse in the entire hospital; doctors don't even mess with her. In fact—" she abruptly halted her speech then bit softly on her upper lip as nurse Trish entered the room.

"Now what are you yakking about? These two gentlemen don't want to hear your gossipin'. Jen seemed not all too happy with the interruption and criticism, and Trish, well aware of this by the stare down the two were having, continued on. "Please excuse her, if you let her, she'll go on and on like that Energizer bunny on TV." She set the trays of food down in front of us while Jen's clenched jaw and folded arms indicated she was preparing for retaliation.

"Oh Trish, you know I don't say anything that isn't true and it's not nice to say I'm gossipy."

Trish grabbed Jen's arm while walking toward the door, "You gentlemen enjoy your dinner and we'll get out of your hair now." As the two were headed out, Trish put her hand up to Jen's face and said. "Talk to the hand, the hand is talking to you, come on, talk to the hand while little Jen's only defensive counter was to push her hand away.

"Would you stop that please." It occurred to me as they squabbled their way out the door; if it wasn't for their two different skin colors, you would think they were sisters.

Quiet again, Mike didn't seem much for eating so I pestered him until he took a few bites for his own good. When he was finished, he laid his head back again gazing at the ceiling and said, "When I was pitching, I had total control over a game. I would determine how much time was spent in between pitches and batters. I could influence a game fast or slow whatever it took to get the hitters out of their comfort zone and ultimately win the game. I'm used to having control Tim and I don't feel that way now." His voice slumped to a low almost eerie tone, "I'm scared." The thought of this iron man—a man once called the toughest player in baseball—being afraid of anything was hard for me to imagine, but now I was beginning to see a glimpse of his transformation to that of a frail dying man obviously afraid of the unknown. While he laid quietly, I contemplated the idea that something changes in all of us when faced with our own mortality. The moment we realize our time is limited, it seems to instinctively alter our perspective as if something inside us needs to prepare for what is to come, deeply examining the relevance and contributions of our existence.

CHAPTER 3

"Tim," Mike spoke again after lying with his eyes closed for a bit, "could you turn down some of the lights for me please." His voice sounded as if it was being smothered and I was afraid his attitude was changing to that of a subjugated man making a final request, not the fiery fight for life I hoped to see.

"Sure Mike," I hopped up and dimmed the lighting to something close to dusk, hopefully more conducive for a wiped out Mike to fall asleep in. I slipped back comfortably in the chair and was caught off guard with his next question.

"Tim, would you tell me about your dad." It was unexpected, but I internally reminded myself I did bring the subject up when we met this morning.

"Well, I'm not sure where to begin."

"No, I mean tell me about how your dad died and how old were you?" Mike's curiosity was very specific and his focus on death once again set into motion the grumbling and sick feeling in my stomach which had finally settled. I hadn't thought much about my father in years being a difficult subject for me to talk about; but I didn't mind right now, maybe it was about time I did. Note to self: Don't start blubbering in front of Mike while delivering his request.

"I had just turned thirteen when it happened, there used to be a little tavern down on Twelfth Avenue, about five blocks from our house, and this is where my dad did most of his drinking. The ironic reasoning for staying close to home was of course if he had a few too many, he could walk home. Although he did drink regularly, my memory of him was that of a good father. He was kind to my mother and loved her very much and not once do I remember him raising a hand in anger in our home. People generally assume because he was an alcoholic, he must have been abusive and that wasn't the case." I noticed myself getting off track and defending my father the way I used to whenever I spoke of him. "Well anyway, it was Christmas Eve and my dad assured me he'd be home by six and was always true to his word. Mom had been preparing a turkey for dinner, and I was anxiously awaiting the promised opportunity to open one present. My dad really enjoyed hyping Christmas for me and spoiled me to the best of his ability considering his income and addiction. Being an only child due to my mother's inability to have more, made both of them obsessively dawdle over me. When he was leaving to walk home that evening, someone lost control of their car on the ice and hit my dad on the sidewalk right in front of the bar. It was simply an accident, my dad was in the wrong place at exactly the wrong time. I wondered many times whether it was a random coincidence or if destiny had predetermined a fate for my dad that couldn't be undone, either way I guess I'll never know. What I do know is that it devastated me. I loved my dad very much. At that very young age, I remember contemplating the existence of God and if he loved us, why do these things happen?"

I found it easier telling my story to the floor feeling a little embarrassed, knowing Mike could tell I had to pull back on the reins to stay in control of my emotions. "Well that's what happened, did you want to hear anything else?" I turned my attention to Mike dazed and nonresponsive. "Are you okay, you're kind of pale? Do you want me to call one of the nurses?"

His eyes fluttered and head shook as he snapped out of his fixed gaze. "No Tim I'm fine, I was just taking in your story," he finally answered as he wiped a slight drool from his bottom lip. The bazaar expression on his face had me intensely puzzled, believing there was more to the facial appearance than he was sharing.

"I'm sorry, I didn't mean to listen in." It was Henry the orderly standing by the door in the dim light, he must have slipped in unnoticed while I was talking. "I came in quietly in case Mike was sleeping, is everyone okay?" he asked while walking to the end of the bed." We both nodded as if we were fine, giving the socially accepted answer but not really meaning it. "In that case, would you mind Tim if I responded to your question, the one about God?"

"Not at all," I said with Mike in agreement. I could tell we both sensed Henry's sincerity and warmth, he was the kind of person you wanted to welcome in.

"My dad," Henry began, "couldn't get us to church much when I was growing up due to us living so far out of town; but every Sunday evening with our family gathered, he would read from the Bible. I considered him a spiritual fountain, flowing with knowledge and wise answers whenever one of us, his seven children, would have a question. I have seen a lot of tragedy, pain, and death over the years I've been at this hospital and at times I reflect on that very same question. 'Why do these things happen?' I asked it of my dad the day of my younger brother's funeral. He died of pneumonia during an extra cold winter we had, one day a healthy vibrant boy and a few days later…he was gone. My dad said to me with a calm conviction, 'Son, I'm going to miss your younger brother very much. You know I love each of you with all my heart, but at the same time I know some day I'm going to see him again.' The Lord's messenger, the Holy Ghost, whispered it to my soul and now I know it beyond the shadow of a doubt. God knows what's best for each of us to grow and learn while we're here. As individuals, we must carry different burdens and suffer different pains, but one part of that plan we eventually all have to experience is death. We would not comprehend joy if there was no sorrow, we could not understand good if there was no evil. You must have faith my son and believe in what you do not see and sometimes what you don't understand. If you do this, I promise you'll be able to maneuver around heartache and find happiness regardless of what obstacles are placed in your road of life."

Henry walked around and sat on Mike's bed in between us and continued. "I remember his words as clear as the day he filled my heart with them and they still ring true, and by the way Tim, there are no coincidences." Henry gave us both a pat on the shoulder and popped up with his hands together suddenly infused with vigor. I could feel Henry's enthusiasm and it appeared to be contagious by the fascination in Mike's eyes, excited like a child next in line for the roller coaster. "Now the reason I stopped by was to see if you needed anything else this evening. Don't tell anyone," Henry leaned over with his hand to the side of his mouth directing his exhilarated yet restrained voice away from the door. "I can sometimes get things for patients the nurses can't, but that'll be our secret."

I leaned Mike's way, "Do you need anything?"

"No, I'm fine. Thanks though Henry," Mike answered in a renewed tone.

"Okay then, I'll be off." He neared the door and turned with parting words as he had done earlier in the day. "By the way, that young doctor and three nurses that you met earlier, they're not only more than capable, they are also good to the core people." I glanced at Mike again admiring the respect and courtesy they showed toward one another.

"Thanks Henry," Mike said with an appreciative smile for the reassuring words. "Please feel free and stop by my room anytime."

"I will, you can count on it," and Henry disappeared in what appeared to be a deserted hallway.

Mike and I were alone again and I started off, "That Henry is a pretty good guy huh?"

"Yeah Tim, he is it at that."

"I guess it's getting late, do you want me to leave so you can get some rest now?"

"In a minute Tim, let me ask you something first."

"That's fine Mike, what's on your mind?"

"Well—" he paused nervously rubbing his hands together. "This may sound weird but Henry got me thinking, do you believe in God Tim? Do you think when we die we go to heaven, or do we just stop existing, drift off to sleep and never wake up?" Mike waited for my response and I answered him truthfully.

"I think there is a God, Mike, and deep down, I believe we all know it, but all the details, well, your guess is as good as mine." Mike nodded in agreement as if we were in the same spiritual boat, drifting along with many other people who believe there is a God but have no direction beyond that.

"I think you're right Tim, deep down we all know there's something more out there and whenever people are faced with death, they always ask God to either save them or forgive them. Years ago, I was in a convenience store with a friend and fellow ballplayer that I won't name, but had always claimed to be an atheist. A man came in with a gun as we were standing at the counter and demanded money from the clerk. He pointed the gun at my buddy's head and told the clerk if he didn't hurry, he was going to shoot him. At that moment, I think the three of us truly believed he wanted to kill someone.

"My friend closed his eyes and quietly said, 'Oh please God, I'm not ready yet.' Later, after we left unharmed and had time to calm down, I asked him about what he said. 'I thought you didn't believe in any higher power?' I had to give him a hard time because of course that's what I do and thankfully we were both okay, but I'll never forget the way he looked at me and what he said. 'I did too,' he told me, 'but when I thought I was going to die, I instinctively cried out like a child would do for their parent'. That incident changed the rest of his life." Mike's attention landed back on his hands repeating an anxious rubbing motion and he said in a beaten-down lowly voice, "I feel like I need forgiveness, I should've been a better father and husband."

My normally quick-firing brain came to a screeching halt and sadness slumped over my big mouth that all too often had an answer for everything. This time, I could conjure no response but my urge to comfort Mike wanted to say something. After a few seconds of reflecting on his personally condemning candid comment, my grasp at not disappearing in the moment was, "You shouldn't worry, you're not a bad person." Mike's speechless internal struggle could only leave him staring at the end of the bed. He appeared physically exhausted sitting with a slight slouch, as if he wanted to sleep but growing into his new and heavy circumstances seemed to be the catalyst propping him up so I suggested again. "How about you get some rest now and I'll see you in the morning."

"You're coming back?" he expressed as a question furnished with actual surprise, which hurt my feelings again.

"Of course, I'm coming back and don't pretend like you don't want me to."

"Maybe they should put me out of my misery now," and he still found the strength to zing me, then followed up with a playful smile which partially stymied the hurt.

"Very funny, you're not getting rid of me that easy you old has-been." I left walking slowly down the hall and into the elevator in deep thought of the time spent with Mike today. The doors closed and in the aloneness and hush of the gradual descent I uttered, "Lord, if you're out there and can hear me, please do what you can for the greatest pitcher who ever lived, oh and he's a pretty good guy too, thanks Lord."

CHAPTER 4

The next morning, I arrived bearing gifts, "Hey, good morning buddy," I poked my head in to see Mike sitting up in bed.

"I guess you weren't kidding when you said you were coming back." He appeared to be in good spirits this morning as indicated by the instant jab.

"Hey now, that's no way to treat a man with a one-pound breakfast burrito with your name on it, I grabbed it on the way over worried you may have gnawed your leg off by now."

"Give me that," Mike snatched it from my hands as I came within arm's reach and doing so with a magical food twinkle in his eyes. He lit up like a Christmas tree every time food was spoken of and even more so if the eats were nearby. He noticed my facial expression watching him devour the burrito and responded defensively. "I'm a big guy and I need to eat, they only give me kiddie size portions in here. If my heart doesn't go out first, I'll die of starvation." I didn't want to tell him he didn't look like he'd be starving anytime soon so I decided to change the subject, and begin phase one of my plan.

"Look what else I brought," holding up a game of checkers.

"What?" Mike snickered at me with a piece of tortilla hanging from his mouth. "You just like to lose at stuff huh? You probably didn't realize in your game selection I was the checker champion in my sixth grade class."

"Whatever dude, I'm guessing you were the garbage disposal champion too." I gave Mike a gloating smile knowing he wanted to return my cut but couldn't with too much food in his mouth. What he didn't know was that I really wanted to distract him with a game while I stuck my nose in his personal family history to find out what I could about his son and knowing his competitive nature, I figured it would be easier to extract information this way.

Mike took a deep breath catching up on his air and momentarily picked at his teeth while unwrapping the other half of his burrito. "Set 'em up young buck, I'm going to smoke you as soon as I'm through eatin'."

The nice nurse Trish entered the room. "Nurse Trish, what are you doing here so early, it's only nine o'clock, I thought you didn't start until ten?" My small talk was ignored; apparently, her food radar had picked up a scent before coming in.

Mimicking a hawk with talons ready she swooped in, "Oh no you don't," and headed straight for Mike's burrito.

"Come on," Mike whimpered as the tasty food left his hands. "No, no, no, there's still half a burrito left," he tried giving her sad puppy dog eyes but all the grease around and dripping from his mouth wasn't helping his case.

"This is not what you need right now," she wagged her finger at Mike then turned to me silently pretending innocence while gazing out the window. "What kind of son are you, bringing your dad this kind of food in his condition, you should be ashamed of yourself."

"Dad gets hungry," I giggled a little with Mike behind imitating her movements as she focused on scolding me. "Well dad ain't gonna get better if you keep bringing him this junk."

"Sorry," I now contained my amusement knowing she was probably right.

"I'll be back, I forgot my clipboard," she headed for the door burrito still in hand.

"Are you going to throw that away?" Mike pleaded one last time.

"Don't you worry about it," she snapped while analyzing the burrito's aroma. "There's bacon in here," she stopped and turned to us in the doorway and spoke as if from a pulpit. "A wise man once told me when temptation's lure is beyond resisting, its reward is generally without merit," then promptly exited.

"I could resist if I wasn't so hungry!" Mike shouted at the closing door. "Damn, did she really swipe my food again?" his face looked like a dog that lost his favorite bone.

"Yep," I nodded.

"Well thanks for half a burrito kid, would you like to get creamed at some checkers now?" I nodded at Mike again but wanted to get rid of the just chewed out by the principle feeling I had.

I noticed Mike's activity level, "You seem awful chipper today, you must be feeling better."

"Yeah, they started me on some pills last night that cleared some fluid from my lungs and stuck a tube in me earlier which seemed to drain the rest. I can breathe a little easier and it's given me more energy." Mike then, apparently to demonstrate his new found rev, rubbed his hands together in the quick friction creating motion you see people do on a cold day. Then in the most peculiar way placed one each on his chin and the back of his skull and with a weird twisting manipulation adjusted the vertebrae in his neck creating a popcorn sound that ended with him saying, "Oh yeah," glazed with satisfaction.

I shook my head and created a facial expression that clearly stated that was disgusting followed with, "Well you're going to need some of that energy to remove your checkers when I jump over them. How about we go best four out of seven like the World Series, that is if you can stay awake that long?"

Mike replied with a slow up-and-down head nod, combined with a slight scowly face and the words, "Oh it's on now."

Our checker war went back and forth until finally a decisive game seven was necessary. The pieces were set and we evil eyed each other from across the red and black board. I decided this might be a good time to see if Mike was receptive to opening up, and maybe the distraction wouldn't hurt my checker chances either. I'm no psychologist but his response to my family questions yesterday led me to believe there was something terribly troubling him and probably had been for a long time. I had a strong urge to prod him into talking about it, and wanted to know for myself if there was a way I could help. Mike first contacted nurses' central station to let them know he was unplugging some wires to tend to his bathroom needs. I reflected back to a job I had, working in an assisted living facility and around many elderly people near their end, from all walks of life. Always being curious with human nature gave me pause to listen intently to the old and lonely, opening and reading from their own book of life. I had made many friends who confided in me by sharing the sad and sometimes tragic parts of the various chapters of their past, and I began to notice a common denominator among them. With death on the horizon, many were searching for reconciliation and sometimes agonizing for redemption. They had an overwhelming tug to try and make things right or at least found a cleansing that came from confessing their mistakes to anyone who was willing and cared enough to hear them. I knew there was something Mike wanted or even needed to get off his chest, but forthcoming was probably not in line ahead of pride. I know most men aren't always comfortable sharing their emotions especially with other men. I've always been secure with being open and honest mostly because I never gave a crap what other people thought. At times in my life, others have jokingly labeled me a female in the sharing of emotions and chatterbox department. Right now I figured whatever it takes, my intuition was telling me he was carrying a heavy burden.

Mike returned a little lighter and got settled back in bed and before he had a chance to think about a first move on the board I started in with, "So Mike what happened with you and your ex-wife, when did you guys split up?"

"Awe hell," he leaned back, crossed his arms and gave me a stubborn little boy look. "Do you really want to talk about that?"

"Come on," I tried my coaxing voice, "what have you got to lose? It might do you some good to talk; besides, I got my psychiatric license out of a Cracker Jack box the other day and I want to try it out on you."

"Yeah right, and I can see you're not going to let this go are you?"

"Nope," I gave him my own version of a sinister grin.

"I should call you Dr. Pitbull, when you latch on to something you don't want to let it go." I could see him rationalizing in his head it was going to be easier to start talking than argue and he knew he owed me one since asking about my dad.

Mike reluctantly eased into his story. "Well, we split up shortly after I retired. I got depressed and didn't quite know what to do with myself; baseball had been my whole life. Besides, the card shows they had us retired old farts attending, all I did was hang around the house. My wife Rachel and I—" Mike paused putting some thought into what he was about to say, "We started arguing and fighting all the time. This went on for about a year, finally sick to death of it, I packed my stuff and left." Mike offered me a smile that seemed to have a deep rooted sorrow attached, and I could see the beginning of a crack formation in his emotional dam. "For some reason I thought I'd be happier without her, and when she never asked me to come back, I thought she was happier without me, a year later we were divorced." Mike leaned over to his tray and poured himself a cup of water, took a drink, cleared his throat then continued. "I still saw our son Chris quite a bit through his teenage years and once in a while, she and I would sit together at one of his games, it felt so good like we were a family again. Several years after our divorce, I had planned to tell her that I still loved her and wanted to be back together, but one night dropping Chris off, I saw a man leaving the house and thought she had a boyfriend." Mike's face turned flush, he made a fist with his right hand and I could clearly see his outward pain collapsing to inward anger. "I got so damn jealous, I couldn't stand the thought of her being with another man so I never told her how I felt and we stayed divorced." Mike unclenched his hand and got another drink. "I did the regular father-son things with Chris but tried to talk to her as little as possible, only because it hurt when I did. I found out later the man leaving the house that night was the only date she had ever been on…it was my stupid jealousy, she was the only woman I've ever loved." Mike didn't say anything else while staring down at his cup. It was now awkward and once again my urge to comfort him poked at me.

"Wow, I'm sorry Mike that's very sad." I knew it was gut wrenching for him to talk about and weird for me to hear but I'm glad he did. Sharing his painful past under these strenuous circumstances felt natural, even a little spiritual, and there was going to be no petty judgments or accusations on this day bearing our souls. We both knew men didn't normally talk to each other like this, but I could tell Mike trusted me and I wanted it that way. For some strange reason, I had a connection to Mike like family, and I knew he could feel my commitment and understanding.

Mike began shaking his head, "you think that was sad huh? I haven't even got to the sad part yet."

"What?" I gave Mike a half smile waiting for one of his jokes to follow but his eyes told me he wasn't kidding and that induced in me the proverbial chill that went up my spine and noticed I was starting to have a smidgen of anxiety, like waiting for the scary part in a movie you know is coming.

"You're the one who wanted to play doctor and open me up like a bottle of pop, I can go ahead and put the lid back on," Mike's attempt at ending his story there.

"No, I want to hear all of it," I made it very clear knowing I had to finish what I started.

"Well," Mike took another deep breath preparing him for another emotional ride, when the nice nurse Trish reentered the room.

"I'm back and I need to check me some vitals now. How are you feeling Mr. Champ since starting on the new medicine?" Mike shot her a glare that said I'm not happy about my burrito but his lips didn't have the guts to follow suit, instead he conformed to the submissive patient.

"I can breathe a little better now."

"Yes, that's something we need to contend with, if your heart slows more we need to keep a sharp eye on your lungs. Your heart is working too hard now, if we're not careful you're going to drown in your own fluid."

"That would suck," Mike said while simultaneously shooting pieces of crumpled paper that used to be hospital rules and patient's rights into the garbage can. He now had a clear shot at the basket against the wall near the window since I slid my chair down closer to the foot of his bed. "I always saw myself as a hero of some sort maybe dying saving someone else's life."

"Don't we all," Trish agreed as she wrote various notations on her clipboard. "Well everything looks fine considering, don't forget to push the button if you have any trouble, one of us will come running. Today, it will probably be me, Jen's having a rough day." She hung her head down and mumbled "poor thing," inching her way toward the door and sending the impression of wanting to share her own little piece of gossip pie, so I bit.

"What's going on with Jen?"

"Oh, it's her father. He wants her to take another entrance test for medical school. She didn't score high enough last time and her parents are putting a lot of pressure on her. Of course, she wants to please them but Jen loves being a nurse. I've seen that child here off the clock, with patients, at all hours of the day and night. Sometimes reading or talking to them, at times just sitting quietly. I think she can tell when someone needs comforting or a little extra attention, and she gives it unconditionally. That girl was born to be a nurse, and now here I am going on and on about it."

"That's fine Trish," I reassured, Jen's dilemma was obviously bothering her. "It's strange after spending a little time here at the hospital, it begins to open a more compassionate part of us when things are so serious and sometimes final for our fellow human beings"

"Well, maybe you should be a nurse then, we could use more help around here." She seemed to pop back into her energetic self with that remark as she waved, smiled, and was out the door again. She reminded me of a funny, bold, black female actress from a '70s sitcom I used to watch as a kid, with a kind motherly quality but not lacking in an ability to scold and take charge, and somehow left you shaking your head every time she left.

I leaned back in the chair and folded my arms in a display of readiness for Mike to continue with his story, now very curious as to what could be sadder than what he had previously told me. "Well Mike, where were we?"

"I guess you want to hear the rest of it huh?" I nodded, knowing he had more to get out of his system. He threw his last wadded up paper in the can, reclined his bed to about a forty-five-degree angle, and began again slowly. "A few years later, I was a pitching coach for a minor league team. I had been on the road for several months and hadn't spoken with Chris for some time. I think he was about twenty in his second year of college, I believe you two are about the same age. Anyway, Chris called me one night very upset to let me know his mom had an inoperable brain tumor and would likely die soon. He also mentioned that she wanted to see me before she went. I told him I'd rather not see her but it wasn't for the reasons that he thought. He pleaded with me regularly to go and see her, but I refused and the more pressure he put on me the more stubborn I became. He assumed I didn't want to see her because I hated her, and I never told him it was because I loved her so much and not seeing her helped me continue with my denial and believe maybe she wasn't really going to leave us. I was actually terrified to see her dying and thought if I saw her that way, my heart would literally break into pieces." Mike coughed trying to clear his throat, I could tell he was holding back and doing a good job of it and I was too, so far. He continued but with his head downward now, which seemed to be both of our regular response when getting upset. "I finally broke down, I was going to see her and tell her how I felt all these years. I wanted to let her know how sorry I was that I ever left and how I had planned to ask for her back, but thought she was in another relationship and didn't want me. To explain how jealousy had blinded me, and for a while, I lost sight of my love for her. At the moment my mind was made up—that is, I couldn't let her go without telling her the truth—I rushed to the hospital. I had been in another city working so I had to catch a flight, then a cab from the airport. I imagined while traveling, being there with her all of the time, we could somehow beat the sickness together. When I arrived at the hospital, I couldn't wait for the elevator so I rushed up the stairs. I remembered slowing down as I walked toward the room; I had a lump in my throat and sweaty hands. I opened the door hoping to see her beautiful face and big smile that could always light up a room." Mike paused, leaned forward and put his hand up over his brow to cover his eyes. "When I opened the door, there was my son sitting next to his mother, his face was red and I could tell he'd been crying. He looked up at me with pure hate, and at that very point in time I knew I had lost the only two people I have ever loved. He said to me, 'You just couldn't come when I asked you, could you? You're always just a little late aren't you dad?' He stood up and walked toward me and got right in my face. He started poking me in the chest, 'She only wanted to tell you that she loved you. I don't ever want to see you or talk to you again as long as I live.'" I could hear Mike's voice changing, so I altered myself and put my elbows on my knees and turned my attention straight down into my lap hoping he would feel more privacy with me not staring at him. "My son was so angry, I should've at least been more supportive to him while his mother was dying but I stalled too long. So my heart broke into pieces anyway seeing him like that…and her…I never told her…but I wanted to, and he hasn't spoken to me since." Mike once again inhaled deeply, uncovered his red eyes, and turned toward the window with the sun streaming in. "Now you know the story of my life kid and it's not baseball, it's the story of a monster that will never find peace and probably doesn't deserve leniency." Mike adjusted his bed to flat now, rolled onto his side toward the window. "I'm feeling a little sleepy now, I think I'll take a nap."

"Sure Mike, get some rest. I'll check in on you later." I got up and headed toward the door, but my feet stopped me before I made it out, "I'm sorry if I pried too hard."

"You did fine, I've never told anyone that story, it probably needed to come out of me at some point, I'll see you after a bit. Oh, when you come back, see if you can sneak some food past that nurse Trish will you?"

"Sure thing Mike," I felt a little better with that exchange, but as I walked down the hall, an involuntary reaction crept into my head and migrated from the back of my brain, bullying forward and forcing its way through my eyelids and down my face. I was momentarily pulled into an empty room where I stood very still behind the door thinking of my new friend's past, pain, and regrets, then allowed the prick in my heart to quietly drip onto the floor. "Shhh," I whispered to myself, "real men don't cry."

CHAPTER 5

After composing myself, I left the empty room with a haunting impression of Mike leaving this world believing he was a monster, a tragic story for sure but monsters don't feel bad for what they've done. I no longer viewed him as a larger-than-life, iconic baseball player but just a man—a man whose life had been riddled with mistakes and regrets, and he was well aware of it. I headed toward the elevator with an urge to randomly scream something to let go some adrenaline that had built up with my emotions while listening to Mike's narrative, his very own sad symphony's composition of heartache. A good expel yell from time to time was what I needed when having too much energy or deeply upset, all part of being somewhat hyperactive. I didn't want the extra attention though so I focused on keeping my mouth shut but still couldn't help the hybrid antsy, inadequate feeling I had. *What can I do? Think, think, think.* I knocked on the side of my head as the elevator doors closed. I had motivation coursing through my body like right after a pregame pep talk from my high school football coach. One thing is for certain, I convinced myself on the ride down his son needs to know what's going on, after all he is Mike's only family. Even though Mike may want to call his son, I know he won't. "That's it," I spoke up. "I'll try and find Mike's son Chris," and my motivation found a home—a newly elected peacemaker for the Champ family. I wondered if Chris would even speak to his dad after all these years and that only matters if I can locate him. Upon exiting the elevator, I remembered a line of pay phones outside the cafeteria doors yesterday near some tables where people sit and eat. Luckily, I always kept an emergency calling card in my wallet, a definite check mark in the convenience column right now. Along the way, I noticed the halls buzzing with pre-lunch chatter, people hanging out in doorways anxious to start their midday break. I knew it would be a long shot, but there was a phonebook that appeared to be new and intact hanging under one of the phones. There's nothing more irritating than having the page torn out of a phonebook that contained the information you needed, another reminder left by inconsiderate people. I weighed the odds of him still living in the area after all these years and didn't feel they were very good but made the effort to flip pages to the *c*'s and scrolled down, down, and there it was, "Champ, Chris," an address and phone number. "That's amazing," I blurted out loud causing a flurry of perturbed onlookers by bringing their verbiage to a mid sentence halt as they took notice of the weirdo talking to himself at the phone. I didn't care though, turning away from irritated stares; no one was going to curb my enthusiasm, especially considering how many people have unlisted numbers and how much time had passed. It had to be him, how many Chris Champs can there be? It was Tuesday and almost noon, probably slim at best catching him at home in the middle of the day on a weekday, and once again reality put a drag on my excitement a bit but I was hitting the jackpot so far, maybe I'll get lucky. I crossed my fingers and looked up at the ceiling, something I've never done before hoping if he was up there watching I surely needed some help, not luck right now.

I dialed the number and like a perfectly unfolding story I heard the word, "Hello." He sounded just like his dad. There was no doubt but of course a double check would be in order before unloading news of a dying person.

"Ah-hum," I cleared my throat, "is this Chris Champ?"

"Yeah, what can I do for you?"

"Well, let me start by saying I'm not a telemarketer or bill collector so please don't hang up on me. I have something important to tell you but I need to clarify that you're the Chris Champ I am looking for. Are you the son of the pitching great Mike Champ?" The ensuing silence worried me but led me to assume I surprised him so I continued. "Listen Chris, please here me out." I added some urgency to my voice hoping to keep him on the line. "Mike told me what happened between you two and about your mother. He also told me the reason he didn't come to the hospital sooner,

Chris. He was terrified to see her in that condition. Your dad never stopped loving your mom. He came to the hospital that day to be supportive to you and he wanted her to know he loved her, and he was sorry they split up in the first place." His breathing indicated he was on the other end but still not responding so I went on; I felt the longer I could keep him listening, the better chance I had to soften his heart. "Your dad knows what a terrible mistake he made by not coming when you asked. It's been a tormenting burden he's carried all these years, and I honestly believe he's not had a day of peace since the day your mom died. Are you there Chris?" I wasn't sure now if he'd hung up and I didn't hear the click.

"Yeah, I'm here," his voice didn't sound as friendly now. "So why are you calling me? Are you his therapist?"

"No I'm a friend, more like a self-appointed therapist; your dad's not exactly the open-up-and-share-his-feelings type of guy, at least until now. I guess the reason I'm calling is to let you know that your dad is dying, it's his heart and the doctor doesn't think he has much time left. I know your dad would give anything if he could go back and change what happened, but he can't and more than anything he wants your forgiveness."

"Did he ask you to call me?"

"Not exactly," I knew right now would not be the time for dishonesty. "I know he wants to see you, he just can't find the words after all this time."

"Listen, I'm sure you're a good friend to my dad but he died in my mind years ago," Chris's voice changed to calm and calculated now. "My mom wanted to see him one time before she died, and I promised I would get him there for her. I watched as my mom wasted away in the hospital bed for six weeks with no sign of my father until it was too late, and he had plenty of opportunity to show up. Every day, I saw her weaken a little more as the cancer ravaged her body and she would ask me if I thought my dad was going to stop by today. I had to tell her I didn't know but to give her hope I would say, 'I think maybe tomorrow'. She would always give me a well-intended smile but she knew better than I did, he wasn't coming. I could hear in her voice and see in her eyes that same glimpse of sorrow when she would respond with, 'Good, when he comes tomorrow, there's something I've wanted to say to him for many years.' I knew what she wanted to say to him. On the last day, when she knew there wasn't going to be another, she strained a whisper to me, 'Just in case your father doesn't make it here, tell him.'" Chris's voice dropped off. I heard a sad sniffle on the other end and my heart was trying to break again listening to his version of the story. "She just wanted to tell him, that she loved him," he stopped again. I could tell he was crying but like any man trying to hide it. "I was young, scared and alone, looking at my mother as her consciousness drifted away, her last moment of life vanished and her eyes went cold. That selfish bastard couldn't find the time for her or me when she was dying. Why should I find the time for him when he's dying? I haven't wanted him in my life for almost twenty years, and I don't want him in my life now. I understand your attempt but I'm not interested and would appreciate if you didn't call back again, have a good day."

He was gone and his detailed description of the event left me stunned. I hung up the receiver and noticed a sickness in my stomach and adrenaline pumping again. His choice of words and speaking ability made me think he was well educated, but his response deadened my hope for a father-son reconciliation. I walked slowly away from the pay phones thinking a punch in the gut would feel better right now. Anything would be better than witnessing so closely the pain-filled carriage Mike and Chris have been riding on all these years. I was in such a hurry to assume I could do something good for Mike. I didn't stop and consider the full extent of this scenario with Chris's heart so determinedly hard and his position on the matter sounding so immovable. Should I tell Mike or would that do more harm considering his condition? I continued wandering down the hall with no particular destination, trying to gather my thoughts and upset to the point of nausea. After a few minutes, I passed by a room neatly tucked away in the corner with the door open. "Quiet Room," read the sign above the door and it was empty. Obviously meant to be a calm space for people and a place where I could pass some time while Mike was napping, allowing myself a better opportunity to more closely examine the ramifications of the phone call. I entered the room, a large curtain hung in front of the door blocking the view of passerby's and behind that appeared to be a comfortable living room minus a television. I sat on the couch and sorted the disheartening details by first logically analyzing, then extracting entangled emotions, and finally deciding that even under these new circumstances, my first impression was still correct. I did the right thing. Chris was Mike's only family, I justified once more. He did need to know what was going on and that made me feel a little less crummy. What Chris chose to do with that information would be up to him. I also concluded that nothing good would come from telling Mike that I spoke to Chris, at least not right now.

I laid my head back and closed my eyes, causing a sudden reaction of physical and emotional exhaustion. It was relaxing to be in a private place even though the commotion of the hospital was right outside. It gave me a sense of solitude with the curtain in front of the door, but I left the door open in the event someone needed the room more than me. With the temporary relief of stress and clear mind, combined with the comfort of the couch, must have caused my slip into slumber.

"Hey you, time to wake up." My heavy eyelids raised up to see Henry—the man that could slip in and out of places like a ninja.

"Hi Henry," I stretched and yawned, "I must have dozed off."

"I've been looking for you Tim."

Something's wrong instantly rushed through me, "Is everything okay? How's Mike?" I leaped up. Henry smiled at me with his now familiar gleaming grin and reached around me with his long left arm allowing for a warm squeeze.

"No son, don't worry, everything's fine, Mike was only asking about you. He said if you didn't show soon, he was going to declare himself the checker champion of the fifth floor and we can't have that now can we? No champions by forfeit."

"Oh geeze Henry, you scared me."

"Hey listen Tim, there's some other things I need to do right now. If you're headed up to see Mike, could you give him this for me?" Henry handed me a white and metallic gold Bible he had been holding down by his right side. "There are a couple places I have marked; I think they will help answer some of Mike's questions."

"Sure, I'll head up now right after I swing by the cafeteria and grab some healthy food for Mike, something I have a chance of getting past Trish."

"Uh Tim, you may want to pick up something that you like to eat from the cafeteria. When I left, Mike had just finished his lunch and was intently eyeing the tray the nurses brought for you."

"That big oinker, it's a wonder he's not overweight." I said good-bye and was out the door leaving Henry, sunshine face and all behind the curtain. Puttering away, I gave thought to Henry's mysteriously captivating smile and it occurred to me how it drew my attention away from the original distraction of his wandering eye. I proceeded straight to the cafeteria, grabbed a couple sandwiches, and headed back upstairs. On the way, I noticed the book Henry entrusted to me for delivery, oddly, felt much heavier than it appeared and prompted me for fun to flip through the pages in search of real gold possibly tucked inside.

"Knock, knock," I said tapping on the door that was partially closed.

"Come in."

"I heard you were awake and I brought a couple sandwiches," I glanced around the room searching for empty trays.

"Thanks Tim, but I'm really not that hungry right now. Why don't you go ahead." Mike was the spitting image of the cat that ate the canary and of course I saw no empty trays. I was guessing he had someone pick up the evidence immediately following the conclusion of the crime.

"Are you sure you don't want one little sandwich?" I prodded knowing Mike's normal appetite was falling very short and he did after all request the food.

"No really Tim, I couldn't eat a bite right now, you go ahead I insist. I'll even set the checkers back up while you eat."

"Oh by the way, Henry asked me to bring this to you, he said the marked places may help you," I handed the Bible to Mike.

"Really," Mike appeared puzzled but eager to see what Henry had for him. Mike examined the outside of the book, and we were both in awe of the way the white and gold exterior shimmered in the light with its decorative shiny gold borders that matched the book marks sticking out from several places. It looked like a special edition, if there was such a thing.

Before we could see what Henry had highlighted, nurse Holts entered the room. "How are you feeling Mr. Champ?"

"Well, I'm still alive," Mike replied, with a chuckle that turned into a cough. "It is a little harder to breathe again," he followed up.

"I'm going to increase your medicine. I'll have Trish bring it in shortly."

"That Trish is quite a nurse, very on the ball," I spoke up with an urge to make small talk.

"Yes, she is despite her upbringing," nurse Holts perked up and continued with obvious pride. "Trish won't tell you herself but I'm sure it was very difficult having a drug addict for a mother and no father to help support them. She helped raise her younger sister, put herself through college, and now is helping her sister pay for school. She works a lot of hours and still maintains consistent, quality care for all our patients. She's a remarkable young lady and quickly becoming an exceptional nurse. With that statement, nurse Holts appeared to almost relinquish a smile but then went back to jotting down notes on her clipboard when little Jen popped in with a noticeably frightened countenance. "Yes dear?" the senior nurse stopped what she was doing and inquired of the junior's visit.

Mike and I watched as the normally quick tongued Jen started off with a stutter and finally came out with, "An officer from the army brought this for you. He couldn't explain why it had been held up for so long but when he saw it, knowing the situation, decided to personally deliver this." She was holding out a letter-sized envelope for the elder nurse who finally took it from her but with great caution. Nurse Holts obviously knew who it was from at a glance because it went straight into her pocket.

She handed the clipboard to Jen with instructions, "Have Trish bring this extra dosage in for Mr. Champ," then calmly walked out the door with little Jen nodding per her instructions.

With nurse Holts gone, Jen gave us a distressed, "This isn't good."

CHAPTER 6

I'm glad Tim remembered to grab some food while he was out, after seeing the two cafeteria sandwiches he brought back I concluded they were probably more appetizing than the tray of cardboard tasting grub he missed out on, at least it played better in my mind that way. He was standing and watching from the window whatever commotion had followed the obsessive car honking we heard from the parking lot, but now appeared satisfied with the time spent investigating the incident and moseyed back over to slip into the bedside chair he seemed to find comfort in. Tim tilted his head up at me while slowly unwrapping his first sandwich. "That was strange huh Mike? And didn't Jen tell us yesterday nurse Holts's husband had been in the army and died six months ago?"

I knew Tim was referring to the envelope passing between Jen and nurse Holts that took place a few minutes earlier and the peculiar way they both acted. "Yes it was, and yes she did Tim." I assumed by his demeanor he too felt a little embarrassed, like maybe we had witnessed something that was personal to nurse Holts.

"I sure hope she didn't get more bad news in that envelope."

I nodded in agreement, "but what could be worse?"

Tim shrugged his shoulders, "Well, she didn't look very happy that's for sure," I nodded again. We both had noticed how everyone we've come in contact with around here revered nurse Holts, and it was more likely our first impression of a rigid taskmaster may have been falsely conceived. The picture Jen painted yesterday of her being loved and respected was far more accurate. During Tim's sandwich consumption, his brain appeared to be off visiting somewhere–nowhere land, which afforded me more unwanted reminder time that I felt guilty for helping myself to his tray of food. I really didn't need it but my stomach has a way of taking charge that leaves my appetite with few options. The staff was thoughtful in bringing the extra tray that was meant for him when they didn't have to. Some people in my life have more than implied I was a pig and ate too much. I've always pointed to my metabolism and the fact that the mirror and I agree that I'm not too heavy for my age to justify my food consumption.

I started setting the checkers in place for our grand finale as Tim finished with the first sandwich and started on the second. My competitive juices were boiling over from anticipation, it had been a long time since I've been in a game seven situation. It was rare at sixty, living alone, with no real friends, I found opportunities to compete with anyone at anything. Considering my past as a professional athlete and my own unspoiled notion, I would do almost anything not to lose. I was more than jazzed Tim had brought the game. He was good and really pushed me, the competition made me feel more alive and more like living. Tim observed as I set the final piece in place and motioned him to begin but was still preoccupied with making short work of the last sandwich. The deliberate quick pace of his eating suggested he may have considered that I could change my mind and want some. He evoked an image of myself with food so I jokingly reassured him, "Don't worry sparky, your food is safe."

Apparently, he understood my joke and held up his last half sandwich, did a pretend sneeze on it and gave me a sarcastic, "Oops, I guess you won't be wanting to share now." That comment, although cleverly disguised, gave me the impression he somehow found out my dirty little over indulgence secret. I'm not sure how but I did know he was sneaky and resourceful. He put his index finger in the air representing a number one, once again unable to get words passed his food.

"I'll interpret that as one minute," I responded to his sign language and waited patiently as the last bite disappeared into his mouth with only shirt crumbs left behind which he brushed to the floor. Some of his quirky traits were reminiscent of my son, so many years ago.

"Well, are you ready to get dusted old-timer?" and I noticed the enjoyment he derived from continually reminding me of my age. Tim scootched his chair closer and grinned at me with egg salad still clinging to his teeth. He came across a little goofy, but I already knew he was very smart, realizing early yesterday he used his goofiness as a cover. Underneath, I could see him plotting and planning, quick with a joke to distract you from what he was really trying to do. He's almost been able to distract me from death itself and maybe that was his intention. It wouldn't surprise me with his ability to get me to open up if he was a psychiatrist, and maybe for fun I'll pry since he hasn't told me much about himself.

Our game progressed slowly, both of us making careful and conservative moves, neither wanting to give the other an advantage. "Hey Tim, just out of curiosity, where did you get your education, surely it wasn't really out of a Cracker Jack box?"

Without hesitation, he sat up straight and giggled with a double jump stating, "I'm a self-educated man Mike." His confidence at the moment was finding its way under my skin and the smooth normality in which he'd taken control felt suspiciously like he was toying with me. A necessary different tactic came to mind so I leaned back, folded my arms and chuckled, hoping he would buy into my bluff. "What?" he eyeballed me and then intently at the board, wondering if I had a great retaliation maneuver he had overlooked.

"Oh nothing," I threw out innocently squashing some of his cockiness. His comment cultivated my curiosity even more so I inquired further, "what do you mean by self educated?"

He shook his head in the "no" motion still searching for my potential move, "You'll just laugh."

"Come on you made me talk about stuff," I emphasized my folded arms indicating I wasn't budging without an answer and he knew it was more than his turn to open up about something.

"All right, but you're probably going to make fun of me," and he temporarily diverted his attention away from the game. "For the past twenty years whenever I have my alone time."

"Alone time?" I interrupted wanting him to clarify.

"You know, when you sit on the pot." I knew what he was referring to but couldn't believe he was able to say it with a straight face. "For twenty years, I've taken twenty minutes a day to read while I do my business. I've read a dictionary, thesaurus, and an entire set of encyclopedias among other things; I love to learn but never had a chance to go to college."

"Well, why would I laugh at that? It's making very efficient use of your time as long as you don't use the encyclopedia to wipe your ass." With that comment, I thought I was hysterically funny and couldn't help busting out in laughter, while inside growing more respect and getting some insight that explained a lot about his personality. Tim shook his head again but this time with a smile appreciating the humor. I was glad he could take my ribbing and he certainly could hold his own in the dishing-out department. One thing I knew for certain amidst all this craziness, I was glad he was here and regardless of his tactics I knew he meant well. He was extremely perceptive and had a strange way with his prodding of knowing how and what to say, like a sixth sense. I didn't know why but his presence here gave me a peaceful feeling.

In between the moves of our game, I took time to think about this odd situation. I wondered if he knew about the personal connection of our past but was under the impression he didn't. If he did, why hadn't he mentioned it and if not, should I bring it up? If I was to say anything, I knew I couldn't wait too long. Every day, I've felt weaker than the day before which has forced me to think about and try and come to grips with the fact I may die soon. I didn't even have the will or strength to argue with the doctor about his diagnosis because I knew deep down he was right. I only wished I could see my son before I went and wanted to believe my novice prayer offering last night could be magically answered, but only being the second of my entire pitiful life I probably shouldn't expect much. If I had been a better man, maybe my son would still be a part of my life…my thoughts hurt now.

"Crown me, hey Mike, crown me," Tim jumped up and down in his seat like an eight-year-old.

"Damn," I leaned forward, "I need to pay better attention."

"Oh yeah, oh yeah," he hopped out of his seat and started a hip and arm gyration that mimicked a drunken hula hoop dance."

"Okay now sit your butt down, there's no possible way I can let you win. I made six appearances in two separate World Series and didn't lose one game. I'm sure as hell not going to lose to you at checkers." I wanted to believe a little intimidation could throw Tim's concentration off, "Remember how great you thought I was when you were growing up."

"Your mind games aren't going to work on me Darth Vader," he now had a pretend light saber in his hand slashing at air and making that weird humming noise that accompanied the light sword in all the *Star Wars* movies. I had to laugh a little, I think he was throwing me off and he knew it.

"Hold on, I need a time-out," Tim had a definite upper hand and I needed to slow his momentum for strategy's sake.

"Did you think I was going to let you win because you're old?" He sat back down and had an undoubting air of a man who was ready to finish me off. The same look I occasionally saw in my career when an opposing player would step into the batter's box, knowing he was going to get a hit off me.

"Just hold on, let's take a short intermission."

I leaned back in my bed and put my hands behind my head, "Well, since we're taking a break from the game, let's chat."

"Sure Mike, what do you want to *chat* about while you're stalling?"

"Very funny," although he was right about the stalling, I wondered even more about the rest of Tim's life. "Well, you asked me about my family, tell me more about yours. I've heard a little about your mom and dad but that's all. Are you married? Do you have children?" I knew Tim heard my question but only responded with a continual blank stare. At first I thought he was joking, but I could see something busily working in his eyes—something that scared me. I had no idea what was happening with him but instinctively accepted it to be serious. Besides glazed over eyes, his now mummified posture displayed a still deaf portrait of eeriness that gave me a fearful chill. Without warning, I became aware of an incredible aloneness as if someone was caught in a limbo state, continuously reaching out and grasping only despair, followed by a heavy hopelessness and I believed it was spewing out from inside him. Somehow, it seemed as though he was unknowingly projecting intense emotions, thickening the air as they filled the room and I sensed a deep dark awakening. He stayed in a trance for about thirty seconds, an uncomfortable forever. "Tim…Tim," I forcefully repeated several times, "Are you okay?"

At that moment, Trish came through the door. "How's everybody? I've got some more medicine for you Mr. Champ." My quick glance caught her eye; she stopped and knew immediately that something was very wrong. He snapped out of his unresponsive gaze by looking down at the floor momentarily then up at me. His eyes started to swell and his voice changed as he began to speak, sounding infected with sad desperation.

"How could I have forgotten? I don't know," he answered his own question. "How could I have forgotten my babies?" He began hemorrhaging tears down his face, Trish and I looked at one another in absolute disbelief.

Trish walked over and knelt in front of him, "Sweetie, what babies?"

Tim looked at her but continued speaking to himself. "And my angel, my wonderful sweet angel, I've lost her forever and it's all my fault." He stood up with a slight stagger and peered around the room noticeably confused. "I have to go now, I'm sorry Mike," and headed for the door.

"Tim wait, please sit back down," I pleaded. "If there's something wrong, maybe we can help," I tried to get up but entangled in too many wires to do it quickly.

He turned in the doorway looking past the both of us at the uncovered window and said, "I'm scared, I can't fix this one, I have to go now." He spun back around and bolted out the door. Trish ran to the door and into the hall.

"Tim honey, come talk to us!" she yelled down the hallway and even before the slow closing door was shut, reported back. "He's running, he's already in the stairwell." She put her hands on her hips and took a deep breath.

"What happened?" she asked visibly shaken by what just took place.

"I don't know, we were playing checkers and then I asked him if he had a wife and kids."

"What, I thought he was your son?"

"No, he's actually kind of a new friend and made that up to help get himself in to see me.

Jen rushed through the door, "Why were you yelling down the hall?"

"I was yelling at Tim, he really freaked out when Mike asked him if he had a wife and children." I tipped my head down and rubbed my forehead knowing what was coming from Jen.

"I thought he was your son?"

"I know this sounds weird but he was a fan, and now is my friend, and I need to figure out what's going on."

"Is Tim his real name or did he make that up too?" Trish asked as she put her shaking hand up to her head.

"Are you okay?" Jen put her hand on Trish's shoulder.

"No," she snapped but not directly at Jen. "You should've seen the look on his face," she diverted her attention toward me for confirmation.

I nodded in agreement then added, "I've never seen anything like it and his name is Tim Smith, I know that for sure."

"So you guys only met yesterday?" I started to answer Trish but hesitated, noticing Jen in deep thought.

"Well kind of, I never actually met him before yesterday but I knew of him."

"What?" I knew I added more confusion to the situation but really didn't want to go into more detail. Trish's adrenaline caused her a shivering movement and with a slightly frantic voice steered her attention away from Jen's mumbling back to me. "The man was talking about his babies and looked like you just told him his children died."

"That's it, that's it," Jen's urgency grabbed our attention. "I thought I recognized that name, I saw it on the news last night."

CHAPTER 7

"What?" I wanted to be sure I heard Jen correctly.

"On the news last night," she repeated dropping her voice to normal levels with the three of us merging into a huddle around my bed. "There was a family named Smith whose house burned down. It sounded like they all died but I didn't hear the whole story, although the reporter did mention the father's body wasn't found." Jen looked at Trish with her hands briefly covering her mouth, then over at me. "His name was Tim... Tim Smith," Jen's eyes dropped to the floor and she swallowed as if spooked, and I could see what she was thinking but didn't say.

Trish did though, "You don't think he could have?—"

I interrupted, "No, no way Trish, please don't say that. He would never do that, I'm sure of it." The words came out of me in a convincing fashion because I wanted to believe but was I really sure?

"You said the two of you only met yesterday." Her tone shifted to a little more sympathetic, obviously trying to soothe my tension but then added, "Sometimes we just think we know people," and her hand went back up to her forehead shaking again.

"Jen, do you remember the location of the house in the news story?" I inquired with the beginning of an idea but desperately needed some help with.

"Yeah, about six blocks from here that's what caught my attention, Twenty-seven Salmon Street is only a few houses from where my friend lives. I would bet she knew them it's a very friendly neighborhood.

"Could you give her a call for me and find out what you can, maybe give her Tim's description," Jen rushed off. "Trish, could you find Dr. Jim please and let him know I need to speak with him, it's urgent."

Trish turned to leave as nurse Holts came in, "What's going on?"

Trish grabbed her arm, "We'll talk on the way."

Now alone with time on my hands to worry, I desperately tried not to conjure up a worst case scenario for my mind to dwell on. Of course, there was no good scenario here with a family dying in a fire, regardless of how it started. Having a psychology degree from the time I attended college on my baseball scholarship, I knew enough about human behavior to have several theories on Tim's breakdown. I also considered myself a pretty good judge of character and my people sense told me that Tim was not a bad person but like Trish said, you never know. My racing thoughts and anxiety caused the passing minutes on the clock to feel deceptively like hours, so while impatiently waiting to hear back from someone, I attempted to be constructive and fit information pieces together. First of all I thought, if Tim's house did burn down, where was he last night? Living in this city for thirty-five years, I knew the area fairly well and figured there were at least six or eight motels within a couple miles of the hospital. My caregivers weren't going to like it, but my plan already included detaching the many miscellaneous wires in an attempt to find Tim.

Simultaneously, the young Dr. Jim, nurse Holts, Trish and Jen flooded into the room with Dr. Jim spearheading the discussion.

"Trish explained to me what happened, but of course without speaking with Tim we're only guessing here."

"I understand that Doc, but it just doesn't add up. He was fine until I asked if he had a wife and kids. The whole time he's been here with me, he hadn't mentioned a wife and children; he had me so damn busy talking about my life it didn't even occur to me. Crazy and unlikely as this may sound, it seemed as though his mind blocked them out. No one could fake his reaction, somehow and in some way, my question prompted him to remember something. I'm guessing something awful bad, Trish saw it."

"It's true. He looked like a man that just found out for the first time his family had been killed."

"Well, it's possible," Dr. Jim started, "He has, or had some sort of disassociation. It's not my specialty as you know, but I did take some psychiatry classes as part of my medical training."

"Could you explain to me how this could be affecting him?"

"Well, one feature of a dissociative disorder is a disruption in the usually integrated functions of the brain." The medical terminology had begun so I added to my extreme effort of focus so I could absorb and better understand everything being said. The young doctor continued on, "Perception, identity or even memory can be affected. This disruption could happen very sudden or take place gradually over time. Dissociative amnesia for example is the inability to remember important and personal information, usually brought on by a traumatic or stressful event and would be too extensive of memory loss to be explained by normal forgetfulness."

"Do you think if he had come home to see his house burned down and his family dead, his mind could have erased that memory?"

"Not erased, but temporarily shielded from his conscious mind. A scene like that could potentially be so devastating, his brain could have triggered the amnesia as a form of self-preservation. Essentially it was too much for him to handle emotionally all at once."

"So by me mentioning his wife and children, it triggered the memory back all at once."

"None of this is out of the realm of possibility. This is a well-documented disorder with people from all walks of life including soldiers in wartime that have witnessed horrific events, basically the things people don't want to remember."

"He did say 'how could he have forgotten them?' Dr. Jim, please tell me what I can do to help him?"

"It probably depends on how receptive he is to talking; we just don't know where his mind is right now. If what we're talking about is the case, he could be in shock and who knows what he might do." Our eyes all met greeting one another with a common care and worry followed by a few moments of silence and Jen finally stopped the quiet.

"Oh, and by the way, my friend wasn't home. I left a message, I'm sure she'll call back as soon as she gets it." I felt genuine concern and urgency around me, but there was only one thing left to do.

"Thank you everyone for trying to help but I need to be alone for a little while so I can sort this out." I knew if I didn't get rid of them, I may have difficulty slipping away and I was too weak to argue, especially with all of them.

Nurse Holts stayed behind slyly acting as though my monitors needed checking. With the two of us left she reached into her pocket. "You need to take this additional medicine," handing me more pills. "You know you're in no condition to leave the hospital."

"Yes, I know," I extended an agreeable response but only to appease her.

"Of course I wasn't born yesterday Mr. Champ." She then cast a long strange look at me which I attempted to discern but was unable to interpret the meaning of. Her attention went back to my monitor and she continued, "I know you're going to do whatever you think is right and I would probably help if I wasn't needed here now. If you happen to go anywhere, I want you to take this cell phone with you," she reached into her pocket again acquiring a phone; she then placed it on the table next to my bed. "If you become physically overwhelmed but don't perceive it as an emergency, at any time while you're out press nine it will dial me directly, I'll make some sort of arrangements to get you back. Of course, you know what to do if it's an emergency," I could only nod being somewhat taken aback. "I'll keep your bed ready for you," she paused and made purposeful eye contact, "Also I don't think there's any need for anyone to know of the telephone."

"Of course not," I agreed again.

"I do wish though since it is getting late in the day, you would consider getting some rest first. You're already exhausted and this additional stress is pushing the limits of how much strain your body can tolerate. It would be easier for you after you've slept, not to mention it could give Tim a chance to call or come back." I was somewhat stunned by the offerings but grateful for her willingness and ability to care so much beyond the boundaries of her job.

"Thank you nurse Holts, you are quite a nurse and a wonderful human being but some things are worth the risk, and I won't allow myself to live with anymore regrets."

"Okay then Mr. Champ," she walked over to the door, put her hand on the knob and stopped. With her back toward me in a hushed solemn voice, "I'll say a prayer for the both of you," and departed.

Alone again, I laid my head back and stared at the ceiling, contracting a momentary urge to cry due to the distressing circumstances, but it was hastily diverted by my unwillingness to yield. I knew if I allowed one defeated emotion to enter into my current mental outlook, it would only tempt falling apart to follow and failure was not an option for me. While capturing my scattered thoughts and multiplying motivation for the impending journey beyond the confines of my room, I briefly drifted back to my youth prompted by my now failing body. I reminisced of a time with unlimited energy, bounding strength and the convenience if available they could offer at this time. My mind wanted nothing more than to leap up and make a quick departure out of the hospital. This place was beginning to feel like a prison for weakened people with suffering disorder, but I was too near physical surrender with no white flag to wave. I couldn't let excessive fatigue keep me from looking for Tim; he was here for me and I needed to be there for him, wherever there was. With my brain now in go mode and a few ideas to get me started, I took one last deep motivating breath and heard a familiar voice.

"Hello, Mike."

I sat up to see, "Hey, Henry."

"I heard what happened with Tim and I'm sorry."

"Thanks Henry, I know there's something very wrong and I need to find him."

"I know Mike and that's one reason I stopped by, I'm here to make you a deal." In the short time I've known Henry, he had earned my respect and I felt I owed him the courtesy of listening, not to mention the warm way he spoke calmed my nerves. Even though we were about the same age, he seemed older and wiser which could potentially translate into good advice.

"What kind of deal were you thinking of Henry?"

"I know you're worried about Tim, but I can also see that physically you're in no condition to go running around tonight searching for him. First thing tomorrow morning, you'll be stronger and better able to help. If you agree to get your rest tonight, I'll find out where Tim is and you can go straight to him, it will be much better for the both of you."

"That's very kind of you Henry but…," he didn't let me finish.

He sat on the bed next to me and put his hand on my arm. "I know Tim will be okay, I had a prayer answered before coming to see you and was given a peaceful feeling in regard to his safety tonight." I wanted to argue but drew a blank when Henry thrust a final blow into my evening plan with a stern but caring, "Mike, you need to trust me now." Maybe he was right and as I gave the thought of trusting him due process, a reassurance sunk into my chest soothing a storm of worry causing me to concede.

"All right Henry, I will but are you sure you can find him?"

"I promise Mike, I have my ways." We sat quietly for a minute as I allowed the idea of not leaving tonight take hold. Without Tim to worry about for the moment, I once again started reflecting on my own situation. I wanted to talk to Henry but felt silly sharing some of my deep personal inhibitions. He may have known this because he sat patiently without a word waiting for me, quietly, and his silent manner was inviting.

"Hey Henry I was wondering," I started my question as he moved from the bed into the chair where Tim usually sat, crossed his hands in his lap all while being attentive to my question. "Do you ever think about dying?" Henry's eyes gravitated toward the floor as he put one hand on his chin, and I could see he was carefully considering my question.

"Are you scared Mike?" he returned. I guess he understood my question better than I did as I also took a moment knowing now was the time to be honest with myself. What was I really asking and the realization came; I was afraid and searching for a way not to be.

"Yes, I am," I responded, "but it's not just the dying part I'm afraid of," I paused to add something but wanted it to make sense. Timidly and a little embarrassed I admitted, "I don't think I've lived a very good life."

Henry searched his thoughts once more, "so you're concerned about what might happen to you after you die?"

His reply again made things more clear, "Yeah, I guess that's right." Henry reached over to the Bible he had sent with Tim earlier.

"Do you believe in God, Mike?" Henry was very direct with this question and I immediately had an answer.

"I do, but I've made a lot of mistakes that hurt people I loved. I don't think God will be pleased with things I've done in my life and at some point, don't we all have to pay for the terrible mistakes we've made?"

"Yeah, I suppose you're partly right," Henry handed me the white and gold book. "May I show you a few things that might bring you some comfort?"

I nodded welcoming anything that could bring me comfort, "Sure, what have I got to lose?"

"Okay then, open to the bookmark with the number one and read the highlighted words." Never having gone to church in my life and knowing very little about the Scriptures made me slightly nervous, I was hoping not to read anything that would give me doubt and possibly make me feel even worse.

"Ah-hum," I quietly cleared my throat, "For God so loved the world, that he gave his only begotten Son, that whosoever believeth in him should not perish, but have everlasting life." (John 3:16, KJV)

"Now, didn't you already tell me that you believe?"

"Yes, but do you think it's enough for me just to believe, what about all the crappy things I've done?"

"Well go on to the next bookmark with the number two."

"He that covereth his sins shall not prosper: but whoso confesseth and forsaketh them shall have mercy." (Proverbs 28:13, KJV)

"Now, flip to the next bookmark and tie the two ideas together." I flipped over to the number three bookmark and was impressed that Henry had highlighted exact passages for me.

"'Though your sins be as scarlet, they shall be as white as snow' (Isaiah 1:18, KJV). Well, that's pretty easy to understand, whatever I think I did wrong I need to stop doing."

"And no matter how bad you think you were, the Lord can completely forgive you," Henry joined in. "Let me add something Mike, one of my dad's favorite sayings, 'Remember faith without works is dead.' So it's a good thing for us to believe and do our best to not do bad things but we need to do more."

"What about the road to hell is paved with good intentions?"

"Yeah, I guess that would be along the same lines," Henry replied with some well-hidden laughter in his voice. I reminded myself of a kid in Sunday school learning new things and surprisingly not uncomfortable with the book or the conversation anymore. The uneasiness seemed to melt away with something warm and secure that wrapped around me like a thick blanket on a cold night. He pointed to the book once more and I opened to the last place marked number four and read, "By love serve one another, for all the law is fulfilled in one word even in this; thou shalt love thy neighbor as thyself" (Galatians 5:13–14, KJV).

Henry looked at me; his normally continuous smile had been interrupted by a still friendly but more serious expression followed with a tenderness he added to his already reverent voice.

"You see Mike, this gives us all direction beyond just believing, very simply to love and serve one another." It was uncomplicated pure direction and my tired heart wanted to follow a God like this, one who loves us and teaches us to love each other. Henry once again exposed his pearly whites and added, "By the way Mike, 'neighbor' doesn't refer to the guy next door, he means everyone." I could tell he was joking but transitioning into another serious point. "You see Mike, it's easy for us to love our friends and family but everyone includes people that were not so fond of even our enemies, doing good was never meant to be easy. I'm sure if you understand and follow these simple truths you'll find some peace and happiness."

"I think you're right Henry, I've always believed in God but lacked any direction beyond that and you have given me some, thank you." Everything he said not only felt good but familiar, like a place I had already been before but forgotten, and my fear and stress were being erased and replaced with hope, something I desperately needed.

"I'm glad I could help Mike."

I admired Henry, with his combination of smarts and understanding to guide me into listening to ideas that were good for me to hear.

"Henry, do you have time to hang around a few more minutes?"

"I was planning on it," he situated himself in the chair. "Why don't you try and get some rest now Mike, I'll sit here for a spell."

"Okay," I happily agreed and was comforted having him near. He felt like a big brother watching out for me, something I'd never had before. I laid my head back and closed my eyes, then came the dream.

CHAPTER 8

I awoke to the morning sun's warm welcoming rays, lifting my eyelids to the new day. I sat up feeling refreshed and rejuvenated, "Maybe I could unretire and pitch a game or two," I joked with myself but only to lift my spirits, already thinking of what lies ahead. A glance at the wall clock read 8:00 a.m., which astonished me considering I fell asleep early last evening, and I couldn't recall ever sleeping for more than four or five hours at a time without waking up at least once. I made the standard bathroom call while unplugging my life-monitoring devices as to avoid the early morning incident of yesterday involving the defibrillator and a brigade of unhappy nurses. "No, I'll be fine. I don't need anyone to come hold my hand," I explained in the usual grumpy old man fashion.

After relieving myself, I stood in front of the sink mirror and was struck with a fit of lightheadedness. Gazing into the mirror and looking back was myself with the bathroom behind, but it didn't feel like a reflection, rather like peering into another room at someone who looked just like me. I lingered in a long moment of disorientation and confusion that stretched into a fragmented, startling memory of being somewhere else during the night. *It couldn't have been real Mike, it was only a dream you idiot.* I clung to the sink while berating myself through the water splashing on my face trying to harness a stampede of fearful chaotic thoughts. *Why am I spooked?* The idea of going somewhere with no solid recollection during a time I thought I was sleeping was at the very least disturbing and bordering on scary. Unknown bits and pieces continued trickling back despite my defiance and I tried convincing myself once more that under the circumstances, maybe it was best left forgotten. *It was real.* I stubbornly admitted and finally shifted out of denial realizing—even though my mind wanted to focus on Tim—these memories were not going away, rather nagging for my attention. I stood up straight and bravely rebuked my cowardice, now wanting to confront the truth but unable to explain how or where I could have been. I closed my eyes in an attempt to remember exactly what happened or recall a possible vivid dream to translate my peculiar thoughts and feelings of leaving the hospital.

With my eyes closed, I sensed the surrounding concrete fortress and hallway noises dissipate from around me. The lights dimmed and the ground was a dusty cool under my feet. I hesitated to open my eyes, frightened of what I might see or not see anymore. A haunting revelation jolted my insides and just as I had succumbed and ready to accept that my earthly existence had ended, a quick soothing calm rescinded the notion and a familiar smell from last night returned—country air on a warm summer night. I opened my eyes to see a bright moon shining overhead surrounded by infinite stars giving plenty of light. I was standing in the middle of a small dirt road with an old wooden fence on my right and a field beyond. A similar field minus a fence to my left and both were filled with tiny lights that appeared to be small fluorescent flowers stretching beyond my visual limits. I looked straight down the road and all I could make out was a glimpse of treetops caught in the moonlight like giants peaking over a mountain. Down below was absolute black and I could hear things stirring in the darkness. An uneasy feeling came over me and somehow I knew the blackness harbored something horrifying that only wanted to cause hurt and pain. I heard talking behind me and spun around in the opposite direction. I saw myself on the left standing next to the fence talking to Tim in the road, both oblivious to my presence with Tim looking right past me, down the road and into the darkness. Behind them by the fence, I saw myself again but in my hospital gown standing and watching the other two and realized that was my position last night, and this was my memory of being somewhere but from that perspective. This scene undoubtedly was my dream but how could I now be back in a dream…within my dream? I couldn't allow the strangeness of this situation to have more time for speculation, watching the body language of the emotionally charged conversation and me by the fence prodding, but Tim shaking his head and refusing to go forward. I couldn't hear what was being said but I didn't have to, unlike last night I had apparently acquired the ability of knowing what Tim was thinking and aware of his emotions. He was terrified of continuing his journey down the road, not of what was there waiting for him but of facing it alone. His mind was full of unforgotten memories of her; even the most insignificant trivial quirks were safely stored. Remembering his lost love and how he thought no matter what, she would always be with him. He knew she had always been his courage and he needed her to guide him where there was no light. He had no doubt with her by his side; he was strong enough to face any obstacle and together their love would conquer any evil attempting to thwart them along the way. I heard a voice whisper behind my ear and quickly turned again toward the darkness, but this time I could see a small circle of light in the middle of the black. Although I couldn't judge the distance, I could see the silhouette of someone standing in the light. A man in a robe, with his arms outstretched facing toward me. I heard the whisper again but this time I clearly understood, "Send him to me," the voice said in my ear. Suddenly, a warm breeze encircled me with an overwhelming feeling of love. The moving air prompted the reflexes in my eyes to close tightly and through my eyelids I could see the bathroom light once more. It was over and I was back again as suddenly and in the same fashion as I had left. I splashed more water on my face while contemplating the messages from what I had seen and heard. I knew I wasn't hallucinating; the experience was undeniable and spiritual beyond my normal senses. It wasn't a dream but more like a vision and although riddled with symbolism, I believed my interpretation was correct and clearly understood, I needed to get to Tim.

Without hesitation, I retrieved and slipped on my clothes in front of the closet outside the bathroom door. While buttoning my shirt, I spied across the room several items next to my bed. I walked over to the table and glanced at Henry's note he must have left sometime during the night. "Tim's at the Acorn motel, in room number 23," it read. He came through as he promised and I knew he would. Along with the note were the cell phone and another bottle of pills with instructions from nurse Holts. Curiously though, someone also left a brand new baseball. "What's a baseball doing here?" I mumbled aloud with my old fast ball grip tightly fastened around the ball. I turned the phone on and used it to call a cab company I'd used for years clear back to my playing days. I shoved everything in my coat pockets and poked my head out the door to an empty hallway. Technically, nothing was keeping me here but a commitment I had made to Dr. Jim to stick around for observation, but I had no intention of battling my way through fussy nurses. As I made my way to the front door of the hospital, I noticed a remarkable overnight boost of strength and energy similar to a few months ago before I started getting sick. The taxi was prompt and the driver who appeared to be of Middle Eastern descent gave me a smile with a thumbs up in the rearview mirror as I instructed, "I'm going to Twenty-seven Salmon Street and then to the Acorn motel."

Six blocks only took a few minutes and there it was, the driver stopped and turned around obviously confused. "Yeah, you got it right, could you wait here a minute please?" I stepped out of the cab and stood on the sidewalk in front of the charred rubble. It was a cold December day and snow had been falling and now blanketed what was left of the still, lifeless house. The entire street was quiet and motionless like a graveyard and the dead house waiting, next in line to be laid to rest. I could detect a burnt smell in the air and desperately tried to absorb the magnitude of the tragedy that took place here. I imagined a house full of love and laughter with a beautiful young family living inside a few days earlier. I struggled to conceive a mother and children comfortably tucked away in their sanctuary as it went up in flames and hoped, as a small consolation, the babies were not awake to see the monstrous inferno coming for them. I could not bear to comprehend the terror and confusion a child might have felt waiting for such an onslaught and a parent hearing the cries of their helpless offspring but unable to save them. An unbearable sadness strained my whole body into a contraction and a long terrifying moment in which my lungs were unable to welcome new air in, that finally released in uncontrollable sobbing. The power behind the intense outburst of emotion forced me to bend over only able to stay on my feet by bracing myself up with the help of my hands on my thighs. Now the painful memories of my past joined in and a frenzied cocktail of heartbreaking loss flooded into my stream of consciousness, a lifetime of hurt thrust on me. Without warning my knees buckled and slammed into the unforgiving, icy sidewalk. With my chin in my chest, I desperately tried to relinquish the agonizing emotions that continued swirling inside me to the point of extreme physical pain. I looked back up at the house blurry now through my tears and reflected on the conversation with Tim and Henry two days ago. "Why Lord, do these things have to happen?" I whispered to myself. The flurry of suffering subsided with the end of my plea, and I passed through an instant that impressed upon me a time and place where pain of any kind won't exist.

I heard the driver behind me, "Please sir, it's too cold for you to be on the ground." I wiped my face as the shocked and concerned driver helped me back into the cab. "We'll go to the motel now sir," I could only nod in agreement unable to speak.

No sooner than I wiped my face and blew my nose to somewhat regain my composure, we arrived at the motel. It wasn't the nicest place as motel standards go, but it was conveniently located between Twenty-seven Salmon Street and the hospital. I knocked on Tim's door, no answer and again louder with the same result. Before I resorted to banging and yelling at the door, a man that I presumed to be the manager exited what appeared to be a storage closet next to Tim's room. He was a short bald gentleman about my age who exuded a friendly demeanor, humming a classical tune as he pretended to be conducting the orchestra all while locking the door behind himself.

"Hello, sir," I approached him with my hand extended.

"Hey, aren't you Mike Champ?" the little man snapped his hand out to meet mine.

"I sure am."

"I used to go to the ballpark all the time and watch you pitch, you were the best," he recalled while we shook and exchanged smiles all while I could see him recapture the memories.

"Thank you, I appreciate that. Say, I need to get into my young friend's room here, I'm a little worried about him, he's been really sick lately."

"Well I'm not sure if I—" I held up my left hand before he committed to the entire sentence and pulled the baseball out of my coat pocket with my right.

"How would you like this baseball autographed and I'll take full responsibility so you won't get into any trouble."

"Well I suppose, after all you are Mike Champ— the famous baseball player." I put pen to ball while he unlocked the door. Luckily, he didn't put up much of a fight, thanks to the mysterious baseball. I let him walk down the sidewalk a few steps admiring his new trophy before I nervously desired to know what was inside. I eased the door open to find a quiet dark room that had to wait for my worn old eyes to adjust. Standing in the doorway, not knowing what to expect, I first caught glimpse of an open prescription bottle on the nightstand, then below I located Tim face down lying still on the floor next to the bed.

CHAPTER 9

Tim's stiff motionless body was situated in what appeared to be an uncomfortable awkward manner, a position irregular with sleeping with his arms bent underneath, back hunched upward and face buried straight down into the carpet. My legs would not immediately cooperate, disobeying my instinct to rush in, paralyzed with fear as a lump swelled in my throat and an invisible tourniquet squeezed my whole body... afraid to discover. A panic wave began to pull me under and I could only think to lift my voice desperately upward, "please God, I can't take anymore heartache in my life." I eased my trembling hand off the door jam, forced a deep breath in and stepped into the dark room toward Tim and was immediately aware of an evil presence that I could not see or hear but it very distinctly did not want me there. Startled and scared, quickly turned to fight and angrily barked out, "You're not going to intimidate me and you're not taking him so be gone with you." My protective command must have won out, possibly with divine intervention backing me because there was immediate withdrawal from whatever had been stalking. With all hesitation cast aside, I knelt next to Tim and rolled him over to check for signs of life.

Upon closer inspection I found he was cuddled up with an empty fifth of Jack Daniels. "Who are you yelling at?" slurred from his mouth.

I gasped in relief now at least knowing, "Never mind that, you scared the hell out of me you little—" I wanted to hug him and choke him at the same time but had to contain my urge to scold recalling again the burnt house and measuring the potential harm a lack of pragmatism might cause considering the situation. I called him little because he was only about five feet seven inches tall, but he was anything but small, built more like a brick house, stocky with muscles that indicated a dedication to gym time. It wasn't easy getting him up; besides being heavy, he moved and reeked of being drunk. But up he came with his arm around my neck for support, and I laid him on the bed then closed the door and turned on the light.

"How did you know I was here?" His pronunciation improved with that sentence, but the introduction of the lamp light drove his squinting eyes under the protective shade of his left arm.

"Henry told me," I responded.

"That Henry sure is a nice guy isn't he Mike?" I ignored the question while scanning the room for potentially helpful clues. After a sharp speedy survey, it appeared as though he didn't have much. Besides the items on the nightstand, all I could see was one bag atop the dresser next to the TV with a few clothes spilling out. I read the label on the open prescription bottle I picked up from the nightstand and recognized it as a strong variety of sleeping pills, the very same a doctor had given me once. Next to the pills, a sloppily scribbled note that read, "good-bye cruel world and by the way cruel world, you can kiss my ass." I shook my head understanding the severity of his words but still recognized the humor and diverted a guilty grin by grimacing instead.

I gave Tim a knee nudge and with a serious displeasing tone added to my voice I sarcastically denounced, "Hey, I like your note, you really have a way with words."

Tim uncovered one of his eyes, "You like that huh, it's too bad I passed out before—" he stopped himself. We both knew what he meant; it would have been callous to continue. Our personalities were similar in that we both tended to be very blunt, some may even call our type abrasive, but kind inside and it seemed we both knew there were times to stop talking.

I sat on the bed next to Tim with an anxiety grenade ready to explode. I simply could not put off asking any longer, there would be no better time so out with the question that had been grinding me since yesterday afternoon. I tried though to inquire in as tactful and delicate manner as I could find, doing my diligence to not stir up unnecessary grief for this already grieving man but knowing it would be a first step in any direction for him. "Tim, is that your house at Twenty-seven Salmon Street that burned down?" He gave me a very fierce but brief stare and then moved his eyes up to the ceiling, a glance that felt like a sword slicing through my chest on its way up.

"Yes Mike, it was my house, and my wife, and my three kids. I came home and found my house reduced to a black smoldering pile with them in it. If I would have been home, I could have saved them so that makes it my fault. Is that what you wanted to hear?" As he delivered the harsh words, his voice became saddled with roughness and I knew the hostility cloaking the poison was meant for him to drink.

"Tim, there's no way I can express how sorry I am about your family." I still needed confirmation to completely understand why Tim hadn't mentioned the fire at the hospital, but I decided not to pursue that direction at this time; rather focus my effort of helping him in the here and now with the information I currently held.

"Tim, a strange thing happened to me this morning that I couldn't even begin to explain, but it has something to do with the reason you didn't die in that fire." I chose not to mention the dreams right now and chance losing credibility with him thinking I was either lying or going crazy. His current ceiling stare continued and I searched my mind for an avenue of convincing in a critical hope he would listen to me.

"Mike, my family just died and I'm responsible," with that statement he reached over and grabbed the bottle of pills, replacing the lid and holding them tightly in his hands while turning onto his right side away from me.

"Tim please, if you would trust me, there's some reason you're still here. I think maybe there's something you're supposed to do." I didn't know exactly what to say to him to properly express my notion but pleaded anyway feeling my opportunity to get him to abort his terminal plan was slipping away.

"Mike, I know you mean well but there's nothing you can do, my mind is made up. I should have to die as part of my punishment for being a terrible husband and father. I'm glad I had a chance to meet you, but it would probably be best if you leave now." Without premeditated thought, I jumped up, reached around with both my hands, and grabbed the front of his shirt forcefully snatching him straight off the bed. I surprised myself with the sudden action but knew I had to get his attention with so much at stake. Despite my age, I was a very large man and still had plenty of strength and now held Tim up with us eye to eye, and his were presently wide open. Even though he didn't struggle, I knew this tactic didn't scare or intimidate him and wasn't meant to. I only wanted him fully cognizant in lieu of a brain that seemed at the moment in complete disarray. I counted on him being the type of person that would respect his elders and not hit an old man, something lost in our society, but not with him.

"I am begging you to listen to me," I let go but continued to hunt for the right words. He willingly sat down on the edge of the bed while I knelt down on one knee in front of him and placed my hand on his arm. We were face to face again with neither of us turning away, our emotions completely exposed for the other to see. My immediate impression of Tim as he sat in quiet surrender looking at me was that of a hollow empty shell with my voice echoing off his inner walls, not caring one way or another if I picked him up or dropped him on his head. My compassion swelled like a tormented father in desperate supplication for his son to hearken to his pleas of knowing what's right for him, but having his child turn away blinded by the stubborn inexperience of youth. I wanted his suffering to end, but I couldn't allow him to follow through with his objective. That would be to deny what I saw, felt, and was explicitly told to do by the man in my dream earlier. "There is a reason you're alive and supposed to stay that way. I believe beyond a shadow of a doubt that there's something of great importance that you must do." Even though his eyes were fixed on me, I couldn't tell if any of my words were penetrating his painfully raised shield of sorrow, with a facial expression indicating a continuous mental motion toward the walk down his self-imposed plank. "I can't tell you exactly how I know but you've got to believe me, I'll prove it, give me just a little time." I knew I was taking a huge leap of faith and about to take another. "Give me twenty-four hours, if I don't convince you that what I am saying is true you can always still do what you're planning. If you're wrong and I'm right what's twenty-four more hours?"

Why did I just say that? My brain must be cramping from emotional fatigue with things slipping out of my mouth faster than I can close it. *How am I going to prove it?* I internally interrogated myself already, starting to feel the pressure of an impulsive critical promise. Once again came the image of the man in the white robe repelling my doubt, followed by the words, "Just relax, it's okay," an inner voice calmly stated infusing me with reassurance. Tim's expression was that of a little boy who just fell off his bike, desperately holding back not wanting his father to see him cry.

"Help me believe Mike," his eyes started to fill which prompted mine to follow. "Make me believe, because right now I want nothing more than to die. I'm not even scared. I just don't want to be here anymore." I couldn't help but to put my arms around him as he let go with a devastation inspired, deep painful cry and I strained to keep from joining him, it was his time. I figured it was his first baby step in healing, to vent some hurt with many more steps to follow if I could only keep him alive.

After a short period, I asked him in a soft voice, "Would you please share with me everything that happened?" I stood up and planted myself in a chair next to a table behind me a couple of feet. I wanted to give him a little space hoping it would be more conducive to opening up. He wiped his soggy eyes along with the red blotchy skin covering his heartbroken face and began.

"Three days ago on Sunday shortly after dinner, I went to the bar where I sometimes hang out; the evening football game was on. I frequently used sports as an excuse to get out of the house and have a few drinks. Neither my wife nor I thought it was appropriate to set the example of drinking alcohol around the children, so I'd leave. I couldn't blame her for wanting me to quit, she grew up with a father who was an irresponsible drunk. She had been after me for years to stop altogether and I always agreed; I just didn't know how. It was only recently I told her the truth," his words dropped off.

"What was the truth Tim?"

"That I only wanted alcohol when I'm depressed. Recently, I started visiting a psychiatrist to talk about my trials of trying to quit and the depression that sparked my urges, all the things I haven't been able to work out on my own. After a couple meetings, he pointed to many signs indicating a strong possibility I was bipolar which for a lot of people includes periods of depression. The way he explained it to me made sense, sometimes I'm happy and full of energy and other times…sad for no reason."

"Once in a while over the years, my wife would be more upset than usual, believing I lacked the commitment and motivation needed to quit. I would come home to find a suitcase with my clothes and a few personal odds and ends to tide me over sitting on the front porch. So down to a nearby motel, I'd go for the night, this time it was here. Generally, she would get over it in a couple days or so. I'd have a promise waiting that included no more drinking, then come home. After I had slept here for several hours, a nightmare woke me, followed by the sound of fire engines roaring by. It was about 5:00 a.m. I left my things here and decided to walk home with an uneasy feeling. I didn't connect the sirens and my house at first, I only felt terrible and wanted to tell her how sorry I was and that I would stop dragging my feet and agree to try the medicine the psychiatrist had suggested. I always wanted to be there for the children and not be the cause of hurt for her anymore by not keeping my promises. When I got there, the house had already burned down." Tim stopped, stood up and tried walking towards the bathroom stumbling and smashing his head into the corner of the wall. I quickly shot up to lend help, "Don't touch me Mike," he snapped before I could reach him. He sat on the floor with blood now trickling from his head and down the side of his face but seemed unfazed by the blow or any accompanying physical pain as he continued with his story. "I heard one of the firemen say the entire family was dead. I became numb and started walking, I guess nearly five hours in the freezing cold until I passed by a radio that two men were listening to on a porch and heard the news that you were admitted into the hospital. Somehow by this time, I had forgotten about the fire. In my mind, my wife was just mad at me and I was staying at this motel a few days allowing her time to cool off. I didn't have any work scheduled until after Christmas and there was nothing else to remind me of them. I became so concerned with you being sick, I blocked out my own life and family. Tim stood up now, turned to me and reiterated, "Don't you see Mike, if I had only been home, this wouldn't have happened."

"Tim, you don't know that for sure." I paused then continued, "So when I asked you about your wife and children—" Tim made his way back to the corner of the bed and replied, "everything came back to me all at once. I'm not even sure how it's possible to forget like that."

"People can block traumatic things out of their mind. Dr. Jim called it dissociative amnesia." I knew Tim had done nothing wrong as he was trying to crucify himself with and guilt was blocking his ability to conceive the probability that if he would have been home, he would surely be just as dead. I had no way to comfort him but felt prompted to ask, "Tim, would you tell me about them?"

He looked up at me and back down again, "I don't know if I can." Then his elbows came to rest on his knees and he started a slight rock back and forth motion, staring down at his fidgeting hands, "I loved them so much." It hurt so terribly bad seeing a new batch of tears silently fill his eyes; then follow each new teardrop slide down his face, release and hit the floor. I sat down on the bed next to him, and put my right arm around and squeezed him tightly. "I know you did son and somehow you're going to get through this, I promise."

"I used to call her my angel, I thought God sent her to earth especially for me. You should have seen us Sunday."

CHAPTER 10

THE PREVIOUS SUNDAY

"Dad"

"Daddy"

"Come on Dad," the Sunday morning ritual had begun with my son jumping on my ribs as two girls attempted to drag their poor father onto the floor.

"We want your world famous cinnamon pancakes," declared Bethany, my thirteen-year-old daughter and ringleader.

"I would like some eggs too please," came from my eleven-year-old Rhyann, the often more subdued younger sister.

"And bacon dad, don't forget the bacon," request with reminder punches to my stomach from my seven-year-old son.

"Tim, it would be a lot easier for dad to get his robe on and make breakfast if you weren't punching me in the tummy."

"I know dad but I like to." His cheesy grin indicated he wasn't about to stop and I needed to move faster if I was to get ahead of my little slugger. With my robe tied up and slippers on, I could hold off the barrage of little fists long enough to switch from mild-mannered father to my bellowing army sergeant voice.

"All right, everybody downstairs in the dining room prepare for battle," I cried out in my new character. This of course was code for getting ready to help dad make breakfast. With children racing ahead, my attention turned to sleeping beauty—my wife—who somehow had the ability to sleep through almost any ruckus and roughhousing. I stopped in the doorway on my way out and admired how her beautiful frame melted into the bed. She was my angel and equally beautiful now as when we started dating in high school.

"Are you staring at me?" she lifted an eyelid to catch her man sneaking a peek.

"Are you pretending to be asleep?" I rebutted.

"Yes I am, and close the door on your way out." She blew me a kiss and rolled over, of course I obliged per our agreement that mom got to sleep in on Sundays.

I headed downstairs hoping to find the troops assembled and ready but was instead given the next best thing—kids all in one place on the couch watching TV; at least easier to wrangle the herd that way. I turned the television off, "Come on guys, in the kitchen." I knew it was my time to shine. "Rhyann, get the eggs honey, Bethany, pancake mix and bowl, son grab daddy the bacon." I juggled eggs, flipped pancakes behind my back, and performed an all-around breakfast making show. I knew it was the entertainment more than my cooking the children looked forward to and I loved giving it to them. After demolishing the kitchen, we took our piled-high plates to the couch and cartoons. After a bit, my sweetheart strolled into the unpleasant chaotic aftermath of the breakfast battlefield. I used my peripheral vision, so I could have my "sorry about the kitchen, babe" ready for her lower jaw drop. This was a regular routine we had, but I learned over the years if I included a *sorry* with the mess, it worked out better for me. "All right kids upstairs, dressed and rooms clean if you want to go to the park." I barked out my command then added a werewolf howl for good measure to send them up the stairs laughing. Of course, it didn't hinder any of the giggles by forcing them to run by swat-the-butt monster lurking at the bottom of the stairs as they attempted to maneuver by without catching one on the back side. Like various mischievous tactics, I learned over the years with my wife to subtly get what I wanted; the children would generally get a bribe with a chore, although I figured a trip to the park would probably only equate to half a clean bedroom. Now, with the queen busily distracted washing dishes, and her back to me, granted the opportunity to sneakily tiptoe up behind her. "So have I ever told you how sexy you look when you're dipped in hot soapy bubbles?" I whispered with my lips slightly touching the back of her ear.

"Stop that now," she insisted but not convincing enough so I gave her my patented back of the neck nibble. "Now see what you did?" she turned to me wearing her playful smile and showing me her arms. "You gave me goose bumps you bad boy." Then came the fluttering-eye-kiss-me look, and we did.

"You better get ready if you're going to take the kids to the park."

"What are you going to do while we're gone?" She reacted with her commonly used hands-on-her-hips pose, then snippily replied, "I have things to do," which really meant Christmas shopping. For whatever reason though she made it taboo to accuse her of the activity most people refer to as *shopping*, she insisted instead on referencing it as *looking around*. "Only four more days until Christmas," I reminded. We exchanged smiles as I walked away, I knew shopping made her happy and I loved to see her that way and although we couldn't always afford it, she did fairly well at finding the bargains.

The children and I loaded up and headed off to the new park which had a great nine-hole Frisbee golf course. Even in the cold, we had a lot of fun and like any games we played, the winner is crowned champion of the world until the next time we play the same game. "Are you girls keeping careful track of your scores?"

"Yes, Dad," I heard in unison. They would commonly drag behind so I had to put them on the honor system. The boy didn't care much about winning; he simply enjoyed chucking his little football around in lieu of a Frisbee. We gathered for the start of our final hole and compared scores.

"Thirty-four," came from Bethany.

Rhyann mumbled, "a thirty-eight," followed with a frown.

"It's okay honey, we're having fun right?"

"Yeah, but I never win." I felt bad for my soft-spoken little Rhyann.

"You won your daddy's heart, didn't you?" I added a big-daddy hug and finally got my smile.

"What's your score son?"

"I don't know Dad, I think forty-something."

"Well, I also have thirty-four so it looks like it's going to be a close one between me and you Bethany."

"Hey dad, you know I'm going to dominate you." She flexed her muscles toward me and was intimidating as a thirteen-year-old girl in a big fluffy pink coat could be. My teenager was extremely competitive and a big talker; unfortunately, I hadn't always been the best example with my sportsmanship.

On the drive home, I had the new and first time Frisbee golf champion riding shotgun.

"I so beat you dad. I am the Frisbee golf champion of the world," I heard repeatedly. Her way of ensuring I wouldn't forget. I couldn't do anything but take the abuse, any excuse making on my part would only make me appear weak and encourage her gloating.

"Wait till next time little miss yak'in it up." She knew to enjoy the victory and title while she had it, dad always came back strong after any loss.

Upon arriving home from playing in the freezing cold, our winter ritual required whipping up some delicious hot chocolate with the little colored marsh-mallows. "Do you guys want some grilled cheese sandwiches for lunch?"

"Yeah."

"Yeah."

"Yeah."

Luckily, it was unanimous which made my job easier. I could always count on good old-fashioned grilled cheese to keep the children on the same page with no fussing of "I don't like this" or "I don't want that."

"Dad, can I help you with the sandwiches by cutting the cheese?" Bethany had wandered into the kitchen and offered to help which was unlike her.

"You said, 'cut the cheese'," I snickered pointing at her and she smiled always appreciating dad's immature jokes. "Are you okay honey? You're not sick are you?" Of course, I was kidding but something was obviously on her mind.

"No dad, I'm fine I just need to tell you something." I stayed quiet and gave her my full attention, she hesitated and I could tell by her squirming that it must be *something* of substance. "I cheated on my Frisbee golf score," she finally mumbled softly while gazing down at the floor for a few moments then up with a quick glance to gauge my reaction. I left her hanging by not saying anything, rather purposely attending to sandwich preparation knowing my silence would eventually compel her to continue. "It was on the eighth hole when me and Rhyann were on the other side of the pond. I had a couple extra throws you didn't see and I didn't count." Her eyes were now back onto the floor seemingly stuck there, and I speculated she was uneasy because of the uncharted territory of never having had a serious discussion on the subject of cheating. I watched her fidget and tried not to laugh until I couldn't take it any longer, being on the edge of "how's dad going to react" for ten seconds was long enough.

"Come here, honey," I gave her a big hug and could feel her exhale of relief. I held her face in my hands and gave her a big daddy smile and kiss on the forehead. After I rid her of the anxiety, I followed with a serious statement. "Bethany when you cheat, you're only cheating yourself and I want you to make a habit of being honest in all your dealings. Do you understand that you'll be a better person for it, having integrity, do you know what that word means?"

"I think so."

"Well, you can look it up tomorrow and teach me all about it."

"Okay I will dad, I promise."

Her attentive and humble attitude enticed me to reward her with some encouragement. "Well if you only discounted two throws that means you only lost by one right?" She nodded and graciously grinned back at me. "That means you're almost as good as dad and you'll have plenty of victories ahead."

"That's right," her eyes sparkled and up popped her index finger that she liked to wag side to side simultaneously with her head when she started the trash talk and I knew what was coming. "Wait till next time dad, you're going down." She strolled back out of the kitchen with her confidence intact and spirits once again lifted way over her head, and I was pretty sure I didn't stand a chance the next time we played.

"You're not going to help with lunch now?" I elevated my voice so she could hear me in the other room.

"No, I have to practice so I can beat you!" came shouting back.

"That's my girl."

After lunch, we enjoyed an assortment of activities that started with a version of wrestling in which we incorporated the couch cushions, although if mom asked we learned not to call it a pillow fight knowing it would get us into more trouble. We also played catch, games and music, there was nothing like a little "Crocodile Rock" to get our booties shaking. I made sure during the day to give each child individual hugs and an "I love you." I've always strived to be very affectionate and distribute plenty of love, equally. I could never understand how a parent could have a favorite or love one child more than the other. Even though they are distinctly different individuals, they filled my heart with the same measure of love.

It was getting close to dinnertime and we were nearly pooped out. It was convenient at times having a bit of hyperactivity myself; it not only enabled me to keep up with the kids but occasionally wear them out. We finally resided to lying around, gazing and pointing out pretend images in the popcorn texture across the living room ceiling. "Oh did you guys hear that? I think mom just pulled up and I heard she has a surprise." I enjoyed getting the children riled up; stirring them stimulated me in all my happy places. They rushed off like a pack of wolves and waited at the front door hopping up and down with roused anticipation and wonderment. The word "surprise" had a way of inducing that reaction and even the guessing part was fun, but they always knew something good followed that magical word. I already knew what was coming, a family favorite and a must when moms been out all day and not had time to cook. Swoosh, the door opened and in blew a flurry of snow and right behind, mom with two pizzas and a movie. The vultures swooped in picking their mother clean and flew back out again.

"You kids get plates," she yelled as the children sped off with the goodies.

I greeted her as she turned from locking the door, "So, did Santa get everything on her shopping list?" I knew I could slip the bad *s* word in by the swimming look in her eyes; shopping was her natural high and it appeared she had gotten a very large dose today.

"Yes, but the stores were a madhouse," she pretended to complain then took her coat off and laid it next to her purse and keys—a ritual which I adopted as my cue. I knew after purchasing plenty of presents, she would be in an extra good mood which offered me the opportunity for a big wet kiss and wrapping my arms around her with a tight squeeze. Many times, over the years, she mentioned of loving the feel of my big strong arms around her. Holding her while counting my blessings carried me to the pinnacle of mount happiness. Everything a man could want—great kids, a beautiful wife, a modest but comfortable house, and a good little business that paid the bills. I couldn't possibly, without employing a greedy disposition, ask for anything more.

Strangely though, by the time the children were tucked in for bed and my storybook day was coming to an end, I felt the abundant joy of a few hours earlier inexplicably slipping away without cause into the dark depression that crept into my life uninvited from time to time. Not even putting myself on trial and sincerely searching the depths of my rational mind for the truth with demanding honest internal accountability could explain this phenomenon. How in just a few short hours could such delight be displaced with a desolate dust bowl of emptiness.

"Honey!" I hollered from the front door jacket already on, "I'll be back shortly, I'm going down to watch the end of the ballgame with the fellas."

"Tim, why don't you watch it here?" she came running down the stairs like I knew she would.

"I promise I'll be back in one hour." I left not wanting to have that conversation right now. It only added to the mysterious cold hurt that pushed its way onto my conscious shore like waves striving for high tide, always reaching out for more. I knew she was upset but I had to get out. The walls were closing in and each breath became more deliberate as sadness was smothering me. At least a drink could numb the torture and partially disconnect the effects of the madness…a little. "She'll never understand," I muttered to myself walking down the sidewalk, "because I don't understand."

CHAPTER 11

NURSE HOLTS

"Nurse Holts, nurse Holts, have you heard the news yet?" I recognized Trish's voice approaching from behind but didn't immediately turn, instead pretended to be working, having just slipped away from one of my frequent mindless trances. I wanted to consistently set a good example for my impressionable young nurses, and I often preached to them the importance of staying busy. "Nurse Holts, did you hear the news about Jen?"

I shuffled some papers into a bin and spun around to give her my full attention and response, "What about Jen?" Trish had her happy face on so I assumed she wasn't referring to anything bad. "Catch your breath young lady and tell me all about it."

She leaned on the desk and consumed a deep breath, "Sorry, I was so excited I couldn't wait for the elevator." Between pants she continued, "He did it, he finally popped the question, the shy Dr. Jim actually mustered the courage to ask Jen to marry him. She said he was terrified, fumbling his words, and dropping the ring as he was trying to put it on her finger. They already told her parents too and that she wouldn't be attempting any more tests because she was happy being a nurse and that she wants to be able to stay home when they start having children. Apparently, they were very excited for her and didn't mind that she didn't want to go to medical school, Jen is so relieved."

"Wow, that's great sweetie!" I quickly interjected while Trish, speaking much faster than usual, paused for more air. "We'll have to do something special for her." I now had to put my own happy face on to be supportive, and I was thrilled for Jen but especially struggling today to get a fake smile up with my routine battle to get through a daily depression marathon not getting off to a good start. Painting on a somewhat cheerful expression to masquerade around as a person who had it all together was something I tried to do anyway, not eager to bring anyone else into my concealed closet of misery.

"Well, did they set a date yet?"

"She said they would after talking to his parents, aren't they perfect for each other?" Trish went on before I could open my mouth to answer. "They are short, they both care so much about other people and they both get emotional easily. She found a husband that cries more than she does." Trish giggled with her poking fun, and I could see her energy exuded genuine love and happiness for them, demonstrating what a good person she is and causing my love for her to grow with every kind thought and gesture she herself displayed.

"So have you heard anything from the secret phone?" Trish abruptly changed the subject.

"No, not yet. I hope everything is okay with Mr. Champ though, he's very sick and it might be more likely he ends up back here with a paramedic escort."

Trish raised her eyebrows in agreement and added, "Their relationship is probably the strangest thing I've ever seen; the fact that they've only known each other for such a short time and are now so close. Even stranger is Mr. Champ's reference of "not knowing him" but "knowing of him," I don't know what to make of that. And the way Tim left the hospital, his emotions had an unbelievable intensity. It felt as if I caught a glimpse of what was going on inside him, I get chills thinking about it. It's very hard…this job I mean, I love being a nurse but it can be such a strain at times, maybe I care too much. Do you ever think about quitting?"

"Honey, it's when you stop caring, that's the time you should quit." I put my hand on her shoulder for a touch of reassurance even though I knew she never gave serious thought to quitting.

"Well, speak of the devil, if it isn't my almost married midget," Trish displayed her usual teasing as Jen walked up.

"You hush or you won't be my bridesmaid." Jen was definitely illuminating a soon-to-be bride glow as she skipped behind the counter of the nurse's station and had a quicker than normal retort for Trish.

"Congratulations young lady, I heard the news."

"Thank you and here are the charts for Mrs. Ford." She handed me her clipboard to evaluate and communicated to Trish with her eyes, displaying a peculiar look and a downward nod toward the envelope sticking up from my pocket not realizing Mrs. Ford only had part of my attention. They both stayed quiet while I read the chart, but I could tell Trish was building courage to lead their inquisition. I knew it was only a matter of time, I guess I expected it from the two of them and maybe I even needed it since I've had it more than a day now and haven't had the guts to open it myself. I couldn't bring myself to leave it at home feeling less distant from him by keeping it close. Part of me considered if I never open it, I'll always have one more thing to look forward to, I can imagine him saying sweet things to me with different letters each day. I can see Trish right now working it out in her mind while biting her lower lip. I've never seen her hesitate on anything quite this long. I almost wish she would go ahead and come out with it so we could get this over with.

"Is something on your mind?" I directed at Trish knowing Jen wasn't going to be the first to speak up, but to my astonishment she did.

"You should read your letter, you need closure. It's not healthy for you to hang on to it unopened like this." We both were amazed Trish being equally as shocked.

Jen was never shy about talking, only about hard-to-talk-about subjects. At the moment I was proud of her, she needed more grittiness to mature into a good nurse even though her new found boldness was apparently starting with me. Their eyes stayed fixed on me waiting for a response, and I guess there would be no time like the present. My only concern at this point was getting too upset and being stuck here with nowhere to run and hide. My chin slowly sank down to a convenient angle to sight the letter sticking out of my waist-high front shirt pocket.

I took it out and handed it to Trish, "I can't do it. You're going to have to read it for me."

Trish opened the envelope, unfolded the pages, and asked kindly, "Are you ready for this?"

"Not really," I replied to her already holding back the urge for tears.

"It's dated July 6, isn't that the day they said he—" she stopped and with a facial cringe raised her eyes to me.

I nodded a whisper back, "Yes." Jen gave Trish an unpleasant glare indicating her displeasure with mentioning the date and incident correlation. "It's okay Jen, if we're going to read it, we need to read all of it," I pointed out to her while trying to still be the strong, never fazed, lead nurse. I had already figured it must have been close to that day because he had been sending regular weekly letters but of course this one never came. Trish continued,

Dear Carol,

The fighting this week has intensified with several city firefights resulting in more wounded than I can remember counting during my eighteen-hour days. It's this type that seems to cause us the most casualties, our boys can't always account for all the hiding places and booby traps. I've patched a few up that wanted to go straight back to the hot zone, not wanting to leave their buddies out there without them. I'm not supposed to mention some of the details here, but I feel the need to get certain things off my chest so I'll remind you again not to share any of this information. I'm especially concerned with a captain that miscalculated some coordinates a couple of days ago probably because of fatigue and sleep deprivation. You won't hear it on the news but a school was accidentally bombed and many children, parents and faculty died. It was a direct hit and every available doctor including myself was called to the scene. There were body parts everywhere. I'm sure there were several hundred little ones and adults in the building when the missile hit. I know it was an accident, but I don't think the captain will ever forgive himself, he's been nearly catatonic since. As you know, I've had a difficult time sleeping while being here and the last two nights, every time I close my eyes, all I can see are the innocent sweet children, the most undeserving casualties. While on the scene, I was only able to save a few. There were many more; I could only administer a super dose of morphine to ease their pain and run on to the next, knowing the one I left behind would soon be dead. The screams bother me more than the carnage, a terrified child calling out for their mother with bits and pieces of their body blown off, not realizing they're already gone and will never see their parents again. One little girl thought she was going to be in trouble for losing her shoe and her whole foot was missing. I'm sorry I really shouldn't be sharing these upsetting details with you; it's bad enough I have to be a witness to this destruction. I'm just having a hard time keeping all this bottled up inside me. I have a couple more hours before my alarm goes off. I'll try again to sleep, goodnight my love.

Hi, I'm back again. I slept for about an hour and woke up with another nightmare and was overcome with a silly urge to write a poem so I did. Maybe it's a way for me to vent, nevertheless I thought I'd share it with you. I guess I'll title it and dedicate it to, "The Children."

We walk where the children once played
Smiling faces yesterday
Their fathers cried who's done this deed
Mothers weeping in the street
I hear the echoes of the dead
I see the sidewalks painted red
300 people maybe more
In the distance sirens roar
Is this what we call war
Now it's time to lay the children in their graves
There's no need to wave
In God's kingdom they'll be saved.

I miss you. Our routine of life, every second from the time we woke up until our eyes closed for sleep. I miss our fun and games, if they all knew what a jokester you are. But I know, I know everything about you and there's nothing that I don't love. I miss holding you in my arms, making love to you then counting your freckles afterward. When I get home I'm never going to let you go again, I will follow you around like a lost puppy dog until the day we die, I swear it.

Love,
Steve

NURSE TRISH

As I finished reading the letter, nurse Holts stood silently, staring off into space for several ticks on the clock before releasing a single tear that leisurely but determinedly made its way rolling down her cheek and finally caught by her fingertip an instant prior to falling. Knowing everything she's been through with her resolute commitment to keep unwanted feelings jailed and sentencing her loneliness to roam a never-ending maze of dark corridors by shutting those who love her out, I concluded this lone brave tear must have special significance and could very likely be a pure drop of sadness. When I was a little girl, my grandmother once told me that sadness was the most powerful of all the emotions, and the burden of carrying just a single drop that was absolutely pure had the capability of keeping a person bedridden or even worse, death. She said that's where the phrase died of a broken heart came from but sometimes it didn't kill you on the outside. You kept on living. Your death was on the inside and you couldn't always tell when someone's dead on the inside. Without any type of communication from the unchanged stance, a smile began to enlighten her face. She closed her eyes and appeared to be whisked off by an internal force traveling very fast, to very far with a facial expression evolving into radiant exuberance. Jen and I exchanged a glance of utter confusion, and I was even more confounded watching her carefully hold the tiny teardrop in her outstretched right hand at the end of her finger like a miniature delicate flower, possibly the ticket required to the place of her current wonderment. Seeing the droplet of water delivered by her emotions with the moment of inaccessibility, pushed me into a flashback and the only other times I had seen my normally guarded mentor cry. The first being at my high school graduation after two years of encouragement and tutoring; her eyes watered when she hugged me and said, "I told you that you could do it, now off to college you go." The second time again at graduation after finishing with honors from nursing school and a bachelor's degree. What others at this hospital including Jen knew very little about was how much Carol and Steve had helped me and my younger sister financially and emotionally. If it hadn't been for their love and support, I probably would have been left to the fate of many other ghetto children—that of a high school dropout. I knew she truly loved me and didn't help us out of a guilt-induced social obligation to give something back because we were the young black females with terrible circumstances. I know that love, more than anything, is what has shaped my life.

Now, in the same unpredictable manner, she shifted her position again. This time though, Carol tipped her head back slightly and conjured up a soft, unassuming, grateful voice that said, "Thank you," then returned her eyes to us and motioned Jen and I close. With each of us nuzzled onto a shoulder and a gentle comforting hand for the back of our necks she spoke, an utterance that went straight through me only slowing to brush my heart as it traveled by. "Everything is okay now, I know he's happy."

CHAPTER 12

As Tim finished describing the personalities and interpersonal relationship dynamics of his family in an account that included a day in the life of "with episode Sunday," it brought a great deal of clarity to the many loose ends of my curiosity and understanding, with an added postscript detailing his personal struggles. Privileged with the opportunity to see them through Tim's eyes escalated my own stinging, they sounded precious and perfect like the best wish of a good man but I couldn't afford to let myself be derailed and crash my attention into a dwelling of tragedy while currently trying to prevent one. Although after hearing the story, I did move a little closer to comprehend his desire to make an arrangement with death. He had everything invested in them. To him, this great loss currently appears to be an insurmountable mountain of grief. He began to speak again, but not before an unrestrained yawn advanced its way ahead. "You know Mike, I'm glad I shared that with you but I still feel like I don't want to be here anymore. Life has beaten me down too hard this time, and I don't have the conviction to get up. I'm too old to start a new family and I don't know if I can ever forgive myself," with the final part of his sentence shaking, an idea loose inside me. I wanted to find out how and why the fire started. Did he know more than he was disclosing by continually pointing the finger at himself or did he just figure he would have been able to wake up and safely escort them out?

"Tim, do you even know how the fire started?"

He shook his head and added, "or why they didn't get out, we had smoke detectors… unless—" his sentence was forsaken amidst another yawn, and I couldn't tell if his last word contained any consequence or was simply drowned in his deep tiredness. I grabbed a quiet moment under the stress and calculated that maybe I could use his exhaustion to coax him into accepting the terms of my newly formed plan.

"Wouldn't you like to know what happened or who's actually responsible, if not for yourself for your family's sake?" Tim surfaced an expression that started with a concession to my logic and ended in a realization that his quick exiting plan would be temporarily unavailable because now, after consideration, he did truly desire to know. "I propose that you take a nap while I go find out. I think you're tired enough even though you're extremely upset. You can try sleeping and let me go do this for you and for them. I would like your assurance though, I can't prove there's a reason you were spared by the fire if you don't give me any time to do so. If I hand you the ball in the ninth inning, you're not going to let me down, right? And let's at least figure out why this happened before you do anything drastic." I was hoping the baseball analogy and commitment to his earlier comment to "help him believe" might keep him strong for awhile because I was absolutely convinced he meant he didn't want to be here anymore.

Tim agreed to wait for me then reached for the bottle of sleeping pills as I began to dial the number for the cab company and noticing the frightful look on my face explained, "I'm only taking one, it hurts too much right now to be able to fall asleep on my own." This action awarded me some comfort. I figured if he was still planning on doing something bad, he wouldn't bother with putting on a show of taking one pill with me watching.

After using the restroom, taking some of my own medicine and picking up the room key, I heard the arriving driver honk. I gave Tim a pat on the head and in my loving father's voice that had built up in me unused for many years, I gently imparted, "I want to see you here when I get back," and off I went but with obvious reservations.

My new driver was a black man, something in the neighborhood of 60'ish, sporting a gray beard and accessorized with a brown leather jacket and matching old-fashioned newsy cap, "Where to sir?" I noticed a hint of southern accent buried in his voice probably from growing up in the south then living north for many decades. After setting his meter and glancing in the rearview mirror twice waiting for my response, he turned completely around and now sported a childlike grin, "Hey, aren't you Mike Champ?" I nodded and smiled back. His initial excitement dimmed slightly with his follow-up, "I heard you were in the hospital."

"I was," I replied, "and should get back soon but I need to figure something out first and at the moment, I'm not sure exactly how to go about it."

He easily caught my discouragement and responded, "Well, maybe I could help Mr. Champ. What do you need to figure out?"

His voice moved me into a desire to share, ringing with a rare echo of sincerity similar to Henry's. "Well, this may sound strange, but I need to find out how a recent fire near here got started."

"Oh," my enthusiastic driver now hung his head with a moment of reverent silence as if paying his respects. "Do you mean the one over on Salmon Street?" He paused again then added, "What a terrible thing," while slowly shaking his head.

"Yeah, how did you know?"

"That story has been all over the news the past few days and its near here so I assumed. Boy, you sure got in the right cab today, sir. My brother-in-law is a fireman, give me a minute and I'll make a phone call." He quickly withdrew a cell phone, entered a number and in a flash was talking, "Hey Sis, is Gerald around? Good, could you grab him for me please, it's important." He covered the phone with his hand and whispered to me, "She's getting him, I'm sure he'll have some useful information for you."

While we waited, I reflected on how good this city has been to me for so many years. Even after retiring from baseball, I've stayed busy in the community representing companies and twisting arms for several charities close to my heart; frequently ending up on someone's television commercials or attending local events rubbing elbows with city and state politicians and business owners. Most people over thirty know who I am, and I'm highly regarded and referred to as the man who brought two championships to the city.

"Hey, my brother," he was back on again and obviously pretty close with his brother-in-law. "Listen Gerald, you know that fire the other day on Salmon Street over here on the west side? I can explain the details of why later but if a fella needed to find out information about how that fire got started, who would he need to talk to? Right…right…yeah now and it's pressing, okay thanks Bro, I'll talk to you later."

"Okay, we're on our way Mr. Champ, the fire marshal who has jurisdiction over this area has an office a few minutes from here. My brother-in-law knows him and he's calling over to let him know we're coming, well he doesn't know it's you but he trusts me if I say it's important."

"You mean pressing, you used the word 'pressing'."

"Yes, I did. We use that word when something is important and urgent."

"Wow, I'm seriously impressed, I think you're better connected than I am and I never got your name."

"It's Frank and it's an honor to meet you Mr. Champ." We shook hands and I could tell he noticed my attempt at hiding the slow and sickly manner which my hand moved, but he didn't say anything and instead gave me a direct look of caring concern then turned back around, flipped the meter switch off, and said, "Here we go."

I leaned back and offered a genuine, "Thank you, Frank."

"You know Mr. Champ, I wouldn't do this for very many people but I've lived here for forty years and read the newspaper every day. I know very well everything you have done for the people in this city, it's the least I could do."

On the ride over, my eyelids begged for some closure time and I had to resort to hyper focusing my worry back on Tim in the room, and his great pain to motivate my fatigue and dupe my tired eyes with promises of sleep after retrieving answers to the dark and haunting questions at hand. A fog had now rolled into my brain causing some mental confusion; acting like a meat cleaver chopping off my thoughts before any could be completed, causing an obstruction of any ideas past this next stop and how to achieve the end objective. I didn't feel a need to panic, confident I wasn't alone in this journey with a loving presence guiding my way, silently in my stead ending the stifled, unfinished thoughts with the encouraging message "don't worry everything will be fine."

As we pulled into the parking lot and up to the front door, Frank once again looked in his rearview mirror at me and said, "I'm going to wait here for you, take as much time as you need and I'll be here when you come out."

"Thank you Frank, I don't know how I can repay your kindness."

"You already have Mr. Champ, you already have." His comment left me puzzled mostly due to his deliberate tone more than subtly conveying he meant what he said literally. Without time and energy to inquire though, I stayed on track and hobbled up to the front door with my left leg now going partially numb. I could almost feel parts of my debilitated body attempting to shut down like switches being turned off, but I wasn't going to let it happen, not right now.

I entered the building and saw a man immediately to my right in an office sitting behind a desk. When he turned his attention up to me, I inquired, "Hi there, I'm looking for the fire marshal."

"Hello, that would be me. Are you Gerald's friend?"

"Well, his brother-in-law's friend," I hesitated slightly due to the uncertainty of the classification, but Frank was quickly becoming a friend so I was comfortable with my depiction. "I was wondering if you could tell me how the fire started that was over on Salmon Street Monday morning."

"Here please come sit down," he gestured toward a chair across from his desk. I sat down while he carefully sized me over then began with, "You're Mike Champ, right?" I nodded as he reached over the desk to shake my hand and declared, "I'm a huge fan Mr. Champ, me and my dad and grandpa used to go watch you pitch all the time." I said the usual "thank you" and was always appreciative of fans' adulation. His tone became a little more serious as he got down to business. "Mr. Champ, do you mind if I ask first, are you a friend or relative of the family?" he paused then continued without my answer. "We're wondering if you happen to know where the father of the family is. I say *we* because a lot of people have been searching for him."

His remark gave me a frightening jolt so before the feeling intensified I quickly replied, "Why, you don't think he started the fire, do you?"

"Oh no, the fire was a complete accident, we just know through interviewing neighbors that he lived there but his body wasn't found and it is odd no one knows where he is nor can we locate any other family." An awkward relief came over me with the word "accident" but a guilty chastening followed as I instantly reflected on the little ones that were consumed by the house, expelling any emotional space for good or relieving feelings.

"I do know where he is and currently he's on suicide watch. He blames himself although he was gone and didn't get home until after the house had burned. He overheard a fireman say 'the family was dead.' Tim is really in a bad way right now, that's one reason I came to see you hoping I could at least show him it wasn't his fault."

"Well, the fire started from some old wiring in the kitchen wall, he would have had no idea that was going to happen. We also found three smoke detectors on the dining room table, it appeared as if someone was going to replace the batteries and didn't finish. Do you know why he hasn't been to the hospital?"

Without giving thought to the oddity of the question and only thinking of the time he's been spending with me I replied, "He's been at the hospital."

"That's strange because my wife works in the ICU at the hospital and said she hasn't seen or heard of anyone visiting the boy."

"Boy, what boy?" Confusion and impatience joined together to pull on each end of the strap that was tightening around my chest, waiting for his response and in the moment between my question and his answer, an indefinite number of things ran through my head arriving at the instant, I was about to reach across the desk and pull the words from his mouth he replied.

"Tim's son is at the hospital," so my blank stare reached across for me and he continued. "In a coma, you didn't know?" and if ever I'd seen a look of surprise, he displayed one. He promptly picked up the phone, dialed a number as I was pulling myself up on the edge of his desk already thinking of delivering the news to Tim as swiftly as my cursed structure would allow. He cocked his head to one side to hold the phone between his cheek and shoulder to free up his hands while he walked around the desk to lend me assistance. "Hi, Crystal, this is Tom over at the fire station, is my wife

— 1 3 7 —

available? Oh, could you please tell me how that little boy who came from the Salmon Street fire is doing? Uh-huh…Thank you, Crystal, no I don't need to leave a message, bye-bye now."

"Well," I asked even before the receiver was returned and seeing my haste to leave, he grabbed my arm and aided my walk back toward the front door of the building as he spoke.

"She told me he's still unconscious but with no life support to his organs." He then restrained me with his right arm that had previously been my helper, put his left hand up on my right shoulder and turned me to face him. "Listen, they still don't know if he suffered any brain damage from the smoke…he could be a vegetable." I appreciated his brutal honesty in preparing myself and Tim for the worst.

"Thanks Tom, but hope is all we have right now," and with that he went back to simulating a crutch giving support to my left side, aiding me out the building and down the sidewalk to Frank holding the back door of the cab open.

I gave Frank a brief explanation of the whole story on the way back to the motel ending with "He's a good boy Frank, I need to save him."

"We're going to save him, Mike. I'm with you all the way." I was happy he referred to me by my first name as per my request, it seemed friendlier. Traffic had now slowed to a crawl with the onslaught of snowflakes growing to nickel size and falling in a synchronous pattern to create a nearly solid white wall and almost nighttime gloominess. With nothing really left to be said about the dire situation, my adrenaline afforded my curiosity enough spark to ask Frank about his previous comment and he obliged. "Do you remember Mike that Boys & Girls Club you raised the money for over on Martin Luther King Way about ten years ago?"

"Yes," I replied, "That area was in great need of something for the kids."

"I know my two nephews had started into heavy gang involvement at the time it was built and because of that and the counselors that worked there, they were guided back onto the straight and narrow and haven't gone astray since. They are both fine outstanding young men; in fact one of them is a counselor there now, giving his all to help troubled youth." I could hear a small emotional flux in his voice and it made me feel good knowing something I did made a difference.

We finally arrived at the motel; Frank parked and insisted on doing the honors of knocking for me as I waited in the warm running cab. Tim didn't answer so I waved instruction that it was okay for him to go ahead inside, and it only took a few seconds after that for him to return alone, "He's not in there, Mike."

"I think I know where he is." I had a hunch he might get drawn back to the abandoned remains of his house, maybe to leave what was left of his heart, and I knew the mere sight of it would surely consume his remaining bit of hope. "Let's try Twenty-seven Salmon Street, do you know where it is?"

"Yes I do and if he's out in this stuff, he's got to be freezing," gesturing to the weather as the recent addition of wind and late afternoon temperature drops joined forces with the army of giant snowflakes. I noticed the snow on the ground had grown into quite an accumulation, and I thought of the many children who would be happy with such a snowfall on Christmas Eve and the fresh powder they would wake up to along with their presents tomorrow morning. I remembered when Chris was little and how we would make a snowman with such a downpour, especially if it were around the holidays. A huge part from inside me that had managed to stay alive all these many years still ached for my little boy—that little boy that thought his daddy was the best daddy in the whole wide world. I knew that many other people carried difficult burdens of pain through periods of their life, but this loss for me and the many years of strain caused by my unpardoned penalty were undoubtedly the root of my current demise. I was beginning to understand that negative emotions like sadness, anger and hatred could actually poison a body and eventually tear it to pieces. God, some people believe, has given us the power of self healing. I think he may also have given us the ability to self-destroy. This had become more apparent for me as a correlation between my sickness and the idea that I had nothing to live for if I couldn't have a relationship with my son had developed together within the past few months. Maybe something inside me decided it was time to let go, with life possibly being something a person has to continuously hold onto and once the process of surrendering oneself had marched forward to a certain point, we may lose our ability to retreat or abandon our subconscious desires.

As we neared the house, I could barely see the sidewalk from the cab, let alone the house that was set back a hundred feet or so from the street. We sat parked for a minute allowing the adjustment of our vision to pick out any signs of life through the myriad of white dots darting down and to the side with a distracting zigging and zagging on their way. Finally, Frank made out a blurry human outline through the chaotic downpour standing on the cement steps that once led to the front door and the entrance to his once familiar place. He appeared to be jacketless with his hands buried in his pant pockets and head hung down. My now faithful driver friend was already stepping out into the cold, "I'll go get him, Mike." He made his way into the darkness until I could hardly make out a glimpse of two shadowy silhouettes. I couldn't tell what was happening, but it seemed to be taking far too long then the two disappeared with a push forward into the debris.

CHAPTER 13

I didn't understand what could be taking them so long, were they searching for something in the wreckage or did their slow return indicate a more serious problem. I digested the dilemma of going out into the freezing cold to find out what was happening or sit here with the temperature in the cab rising and overtaking my comfort level. I decided to stay put another minute and rolling down the window to tame the heat seemed a better option than trying to reach over the front seat to the controls up front. As the cold air rushed in, I could hear footsteps and voices behind the wind, but their creators were still embedded in the darkness, coming closer until I saw three figures approaching the vehicle. They were semi-hunched over moving along together until one man I didn't recognize broke formation and made his way in front of the cab toward the house across the street briefly slowing to bellow backwards through the weather. "We'll be praying Tim," and raised a right hand signifying his good-bye. Tim returned a wave acknowledging the man he must have known, and the remaining two made their way behind the car, with Tim entering the back as Frank jumped in the driver's seat blowing into his hands condemning the cold with a few carefully chosen words.

Tim closed the door and immediately let me know, "Frank told me everything Mike, I can't believe it." His initial excitement produced a repetitive state and he went on, "I just can't believe it Mike, I can't believe it." He soon regained control of his word repetition, but an eager expression contradicted the quick new calm of his speech, and the abrupt behavioral course change indicated to me an obvious suppression of pressure-packed emotion I could clearly see building in his eyes. I only nodded in response allowing him an open opportunity to release something, for relief, being temporarily overwhelmed with the joyous yet shocking news. Within moments, his composure came even more into focus and any more venting was unpredictably stifled as he switched his attention to an audit of my worsening condition, angling for a better view of my face in the dim light of the cab. "Mike, you don't look very good, we need to get you to the hospital."

Frank heard his comment and interjected, "We need to get both of you to the hospital and that's where we're going as fast as I can make this sled go safely through this damn blizzard."

Tim reached over on the drive, patted my arm and whispered privately, "I'm sorry I put you through all this while you're sick," he paused then added, "Thank you Mike." He turned his head downward to the floor and muttered with a quiet intensity barely loud enough I could hear, his way of sharing. "I hope he'll be okay, I could go on if I need to take care of him, but I definitely can't lose him twice, it's going to take my lifetime to get over losing his sisters and mother," and a small piece of pain was set free with a confession I was glad to hear from him. The life he owned but was eager to be rid of a short time earlier was once again infused with purpose, and his talk of getting over them fulfilled my purpose, and I confidentially communicated a hushed "thank you" to my invisible guide.

Frank skillfully maneuvered us through the snow and directly up to the front of the hospital before stopping. Tim wasted no time in exiting the cab as I pleaded a request of him in his anxious and hurried state to, "please keep us informed if you can."

He stopped part way to the hospital door, turned to look at me, then bent over slightly to gain a better view of Frank in the driver's seat and said, "Would you please make sure he gets his butt back to his room and in bed?" He then gave Frank an assumed and respectful "thank you" nod and lent his attention back to answer me, "I will." After Tim left my sight, I used the cell phone nurse Holts had given me and pushed the dedicated button to reach her, "Hello," came from the other end.

"Hi, this is Mike Champ," and was cut off by the controlling yet well-meaning nurse.

"Are you okay, where are you?" shot back at me.

"I'm down at the main entrance and feeling kind of weak."

"I'll send someone right down, just stay put." Even though her exterior shined of sternness, I knew as did everyone else who knows her understood that the well-disciplined attitude really was her cover, probably protecting a scared, unsure young girl like the child that lives in all of us and stays hidden so we can play grown-up. The few minutes of waiting included saying my good-byes to Frank, and I reiterated how grateful I was for his assistance.

I also pointed to the zeros across his meter that had stayed off during our running around and reached for my wallet to compensate his kindness, but as he became aware of my motive he met my hand with his and opposed fortifying his personality. "Don't you dare," and he eased my hand in reverse to secure the wallet again.

"Mike, helping you in trying to help that young man and that little boy has been a privilege that I will cherish the rest of my life and taking money for it would tarnish my memory." His every deed personified the type of person he was, old school, an understated man that showed it was *cool* to care, a dying breed in our modern fast-paced America. Our shared understanding and admiration moment had to end with my escort arriving, pushing a wheelchair so Frank keen to his surroundings made his way around to my door, and the two of them aided me into my new ride. Frank knelt down and handed me one of his cards. "If you ever need to get somewhere you call, I will be very hurt if you don't." He shook my hand, smiled at Trish, and drove off looking back at me one more time in the rearview mirror. We instinctively knew we would never see each other again, but that didn't change the positive *forever affect* we both got to keep—the influence people have on one another when their path lives intersect and are both better for it.

Trish, being Trish, started our conversation with, "Do you make everyone like you?" then took the brake off the back wheel and added as we rolled along, "I'm glad you're back Mr. Champ, we were all very worried."

On the way back up to our fifth floor home, I was barely able to deflect Trish's questions regarding Tim and what had taken place while I was gone. I had hoped to get everyone who wanted to hear the incredible story of today's occurrences in my room before I shared, conserving my strength to tell the inspiring tale only one good time. Instead of divulging my report, I convinced her to share the latest news from here which included the recent engagement and the miraculous letter opening event. Trish, being Trish again, told both accounts with detailed honesty, and we both agreed the hospital was currently full of the unpredictable and extraordinary. Almost as quickly as I could slip into my hospital gown and back in bed, an audience had assembled themselves around me with nurse Holts and the young Dr. Jim on my right side, Trish and Jen to my left. The senior nurse spoke for the group, "We have a couple minutes, so what happened?" I suddenly felt I inherited something as close to a family as I have had since my son pronounced me dead.

I began the day's experience from the moment I woke up this morning until my farewell to Frank and the couple minutes nurse Holts had offered expanded into several more even with me attempting a speedy presentation. As I explained the details of the last ten hours, no eyes were left dry and at the point I revealed Tim's son being a few floors up from our current position; the exhilaration from the group could not be contained nor the tears restrained.

Everyone's urge was to hug one another, feeling a small victory for our team, and nurse Holts eased forward to offer me a rare smile and words that sprang a small cheer from my worn and weary heart. "You did a real good thing," and squeezed my arm with her left hand as she wiped the corner of her eye with her right.

Behind her, Dr. Jim offered himself as the reconnaissance officer and with him being a doctor was probably best suited for the job. "I have a minute, why don't I go upstairs and get an update on the boy." He left the room walking backwards out the door with crossed fingers which we all interpreted as a sign of hope for good news and his gesture was met with unanimous group approval.

Nurse Holts turned her attention to the younger nurses, "Do you two want to check in on our other patients while I get Mr. Champ situated for some rest, I think in his condition he's had a busy enough day." Alone with the senior nurse, she reattached my life-monitoring wires, had some food and drink brought in, then hesitantly informed me. "I don't want to alarm you but you're getting worse; your skin is turning a light shade of blue which means your blood is not getting enough oxygen, you really need some sleep." I wanted to share with her a rational realization that had gently graduated itself into my acceptance throughout the day, although I was guessing with her experience she already knew but I needed to say out loud anyway.

"You know nurse Holts, I'm pretty sure I won't be around much longer and there's not a whole lot you or I can do about it. Instead of worrying, I think I'd like to try and enjoy what time I've left and I feel a plethora of good deeds abounding inside me. In fact, I have so much to do I'm not sure when I'll have time to sleep." I could tell she didn't like the last bit of sarcasm but reluctantly stopped her busy work and with her hands on her hips, she took a long look at me.

"All right Mr. Champ I won't nag you. You do what you feel is right and I'll be supportive as long as you're not planning any more gallivanting around in the snow."

"That sounds like a fair deal," I agreed as I started on my tray of supper, "and could you let me know if you hear anything about little Tim."

"As soon as I know you'll know," and her nursing duties beckoned her out the door.

With my dinner nearly gone and boredom from channel surfing setting in, a familiar and friendly voice gained my attention immediately following a quiet knock in the doorway. "Hey Mike, are you busy?" It was Henry tapping on the inside of my door already in the room just out of my view behind the partially closed privacy curtain. I shoved the last bite of food in my mouth and set the tray to the side in one motion then clicked the television off and waved Henry over with my next act.

"Henry get over here, how are you?" I was extremely happy to see him and wanted to share what had taken place today, but before I could manage another word still trying to work down the last bit of food he revealed.

"I heard what happened Mike, what wonderful news," I shook my head in a positive fashion and he continued. "It may seem a small consolation of goodness that came out of truly horrific circumstances but it's something, all we can do is trust and persevere, continually pushing forward is definitely the hard part of life."

"I know Henry. I just hope Tim knows, that little boy is going to need him to be strong. I think he'll pull himself up. Tim's very smart; the two of them will find their way…that is if his son pulls through."

Henry sat down on the edge of my bed moving his head in agreement. "Well, I also wanted to see how you were doing, is there anything I can do for you Mike?" I interrupted the flow of the discussion to ponder and we both let the quietness soothe our minds while I devoted a few seconds of thought to his question with emphasis on the word "anything," considering carefully my time draining away being absorbed by each passing moment. With an innocent child's life and health weighing heavily on me, there was only one thing I could ask of the most spiritual person I knew.

"Yes Henry, there is one thing you could do for me, would you say a prayer for Tim's son with me? Can we pray for him to not just live but to be free of any complications from the fire? Do you think that would be asking for too much?"

"No, I don't think it's an unreasonable request, we only want that little boy to have a healthy, happy life, I would be honored to pray with you Mike." He smiled then folded his arms and bowed his head. I followed his lead not having much experience involving this Christian ritual and not wanting to offend God in any way to lessen the effectiveness of the prayer. Henry began speaking in a clear reverent voice at a normal tone that sounded very natural as if his words were directed toward someone presently in the room with us.

"Our kind, loving Father in heaven, we come before thee with broken hearts and contrite spirits and humbly ask if thou would heal Tim's son. He's a small boy that has so much to overcome emotionally and physically. Father please make him whole and bless Tim and his son to be able to adapt to life without the females in their family. Help them to overcome the pain of loss and find happiness along with their health. We're so grateful for the many good things thou bestows upon us…and Father please bless Mike, he's a good man and could use some relief from his physical and emotional suffering also. We ask for these favors and blessings in the name of our Savior, Jesus Christ, amen."

As Henry finished, he opened his eyes, reached over and patted my shoulder with the message, "I have a peaceful feeling inside, I think good things will happen." I was impressed with Henry's beautiful word usage and simplistic approach to prayer. He made it seem so easy and I too shared the peaceful feeling but it went beyond that for me. I felt the same love that was in the breeze that had previously encircled me in the vision I had and a reassuring correspondence like the Lord was speaking to me within the feeling saying, "I heard your prayer and I'm going to heal the little boy."

"Thank you for saying that Henry and the part for me. I didn't consider myself worthy enough to ask for so much on my own, and I really want Tim and his son to be all right. Henry scrunched his eyes at me appearing slightly disgruntled with what I said.

"Mike, I think you sell yourself way too short. Don't get me wrong, it's good to be humble but you're a far better person than you give yourself credit for. Let me ask you a question, how do you think everything went today? I mean considering the awful situation, did things go along fairly smooth?" I knew Henry would make a point with his question and I wasn't sure where he was leading me so instead of allowing my wandering mind to wonder, I adhered to the answer.

"Well yeah, they most certainly did. The *smooth* things started this morning with you leaving the address for me and a mysterious baseball showing up on the table." I mentioned the baseball with an inquisitive posture not knowing where it came from, and Henry noticing my search promptly shrugged his shoulders with denial. I went on with my list, "The ball conveniently enabled me to bribe the manager for access into Tim's room when he didn't answer the door. Of course, my talk with Tim went pretty well with several strong promptings guiding what I should say to him. Frank—the driver who picked me up—happened to be the brother-in-law of a fireman who knew the fire marshal that had information about the fire, and he was the husband of a nurse who works upstairs in ICU. I would say considering the crummy circumstances yes, things went along as quickly and well as I could have hoped. And Henry, I don't believe they were coincidences, I truly believe the Lord guided me throughout the entire day."

"I'm sure that's true Mike and we should give much thanks to the Lord for using *you* as his tool to bring something about, but *you* were willing to be subjected to the required work. *You* went to Tim's motel and *you* went to the fire marshal's office. *You* found Tim and brought him back to the hospital to be with his son. How did you feel today? Tired, sick, yet *you* still got up this morning, a very sick man and ran around the city, in a storm I might add to help another person. For your information Mr. Baseball pitcher, not everyone would go through so much trouble, so I'm a little offended when you put my friend down, even a little."

"Your friend?" I inquired horribly pretending to be confused even though I was pretty sure I understood what he meant but wanted to hear him say it anyway.

"Yes Mike, you're my friend and you're way too hard on yourself for whatever mistake you punish yourself with from years ago. When you have righteous intentions, it aids the doors of heaven to open up and pour out more of the assistance you're seeking. Pure and selfless motives clear an easier path for divine intervention to follow. Your good qualities made a difference in helping Tim. I'm not saying the Lord couldn't have found a way to intervene or facilitate his will, but you put forth the effort and were willing to be the Lord's helper; I believe that work will translate into wonderful blessings for you." Henry was on a roll and I believe his purpose was now coming to light. He recognized the guilt and fear I still maintained associated with death as we had discussed yesterday and with my life's end rapidly approaching, he was playing the role of comforter by presenting me to myself as noble and virtuous. He did make me feel a little better but was unable to alter the normality of the clump of hurt deep inside that came from the memory and mistakes I made with my son and his mother. I would never forget the reasons that caused my son's disassociation and it would stay the epicenter of my fear. I did however enjoy listening to him say nice things about me and I appreciated what he was trying to do, I listened on. "We can't take money with us Mike but we can stockpile good deeds, the true, authentic heavenly treasure and although I am not the judge, my guess is you will not be a poor man in heaven. How many people turn a blind eye to need and suffering? It's much easier for people to justify not helping by saying to themselves, 'someone else will do it' or 'I'll help next time.' For the ones who need the help, there may be no next time. The work gets left undone and for those who procrastinate with the means or the time to lend aid, they will not be blameless. No, Mike, I disagree with your assessment of your own worthiness. You have a good heart, you saw a need and you did something about it and that my friend counts. Remember what the good Lord said, 'inasmuch as ye have done it unto one of the least of these my brethren, ye have done it unto me'." (Matthew 25:40, KJV)

Henry halted his warmhearted sermon that was clearly designed and devoted to lifting my spirits and began rubbing the bottom of his chin as if plotting a strategy, then delivered his deduction. "Boy, I better stop praising you so much, your head might blow up with all the humility from your heart." We exchanged smiles then he disappeared one more time behind a solemn countenance. "Seriously Mike, you have a lot of repentance ahead of you."

His instant role reversal from silly to sober, a previously unseen tactic lured me straight in and I took the bait like a big dumb fish, "What do you mean Henry?"

"Well, I know that big, bushy, brown thing on your face you call a mustache has to be a sin, I just need to find it in the Scriptures," and we both exhaled in laughter so hard I thought my lungs might collapse. Henry gave me a manly hug that included a couple pats on the back and before disappearing behind the curtain and out the door, gave one last praise, "You did good Mike," nodding his approval and waving his tender smile goodbye.

CHAPTER 14

"We're so glad you made it Mr. Smith, we were expecting you," she replied before turning and motioning me to follow. "My husband Tom is the fire marshal and he called right after speaking with Mr. Champ earlier and explained the situation. We're very sorry for your loss," the briskly walking nurse with the name tag Rebecca spoke over her left shoulder as I kept close. Within a few moments and without leaving the same large room, she stopped and faced me in front of a curtain. The white temporary wall shielded my view from a beeping heart monitor that was emitting the methodical, morbid noise I now associated with the carnal struggle people have while clinging on to dear life. "Listen Mr. Smith."

"Please call me Tim."

"Tim, it's hard the first time to see him this way. I wanted to remind you before you do, the good news is all his organs are functioning on their own and that's a really good sign, okay?" Her purposeful eye contact and compassion-filled voice was meant to weave the encouraging words through my obvious escalating apprehension, undoubtedly to ease my inevitable distress. "Do you have any questions for me before I go back to the nurse's station?" she asked while pointing back to the counter we just came from, before continuing. "I apologize but we had an urgent matter in another area and the other nurse had to leave for a few minutes, and I'm the only one here." I focused long enough to hear her reasoning and understand her rationale, but an accumulation of nervousness caused my unsteady attention to escape her control. I noticed eight other curtains in the room, four on each side of our current position spread out in a horse shoe pattern and a myriad of beeps coming from all directions like a symphony of crickets eerily chirping a death concert.

With ascending adrenaline igniting an enhanced alertness, my fixation was drawn away from the beeps and to a boom, boom, pounding in my chest and a dry swelling throat as I anticipated seeing my son lying behind…behind…. "The damn thing in my way," I murmured as I turned away from her. Not able to withstand another wrenching second of delay, I leaped into the impending moment jerking back the obstruction and rushed to my boy trampling the emotional blockage on the way. I stood over him and instinctively stroked his hair and kissed his forehead feeling fight now more than a fear, believing I would not let anyone or anything take him away. My primitive urge was to hover over him to ensure his safety with nothing in the universe powerful enough to get through my body's inspired physical shelter or around a newly formed barrier of love.

"Daddy won't let anything happen to you ever again I promise," I whispered to my son's ear hour after hour late into the night.

"Hey, kiddo," accompanied a gentle nudge and I awoke in the chair next to my son with my head resting on the edge of the bed next to his pillow and left arm draped over his body as Mike, the apparent nudger, sat in a wheelchair in front of me.

"Hey, Mike," I grumbled dislodging mucus from my throat and despite being disorientated, I took notice the lights had been dimmed. To disperse a haze blocking cognitive clarity, I employed a vigorous head shake while inhaling a large quantity of oxygen through a yawn thus clearing most of the cobwebs, and liberating an earlier commitment to try and keep Mike informed. "There hasn't been any change in his condition… I'm sorry I didn't let you know…it's just when I saw him…I was afraid to leave." We both recognized my choppy sentence as a good barometer and beginning signs of an increase in emotional instability caused by the excruciating circumstances resurfacing to a sharp recollection after lying buried in a deep, overdue sleep.

Mike quickly leaned over again, "Just relax Tim, it's fine. I have spies keeping me informed anyway," his smile and pat on my knee calmed the rising. Mike sat himself up taller to gain a better view of my son over the bed railing and commented, "He is a beautiful boy Tim and he's going to be all right, I know he's going to be all right." I responded with a half smile and nod appreciating his sincerity and visible conviction in which he confidently stated his opinion as a matter of fact. It brought a great deal of encouragement to aid in bolstering my insecure hope knowing that Mike had previously been very right before when displaying such faith in his predictions. "Oh, it may not be the best time to say this but Merry Christmas," he added. I had mostly forgotten during the week that today was Christmas, giving much thought to the holy holiday that involved presents, joy, and love without my family only added to the incredible hurt. We sat alone a minute in the quiet with only the harassing, incessant beeps with their constant pinging, repeatedly stabbing the notion into my brain that they were in charge and presently replacing the child's laughter. To mutiny against the irritating continual reminder, I pulled my attention switch onto Mike and how he was feeling, but he was at the very least impersonating a man in better shape than when I saw him last, so I withdrew the question from my mind. We were both a little uncomfortable with no dialogue and Mike spoke first beating me to words by giving casual mention, "I just woke up from the strangest dream."

I recognized this as an opportunity for us to perpetuate more conversation, and I wanted to show Mike I cared and appreciated him so I instantly offered to hear, "Tell me about it."

"Well," Mike began but not without examining my true level of interest as a dream listener with a slightly suspicious overtone and displaying an inquisitive facial pose. To help sway his analysis, I prepared myself to be genuinely attentive by leaning in with my elbows propped up on my knees angled toward him like an antenna and Mike being content with this gesture began. "I dreamt I had been on an extended road trip with the baseball team and hadn't seen my wife in what seemed an eternity, so long that many of the small details about her were starting to fade away. I sat waiting to board a plane for a long period after the flight had already been delayed several times. I heard a pay phone that was next to me ring so I reached over and answered it, it was my wife. I told her how much I missed her and loved her, and I was sorry for being gone for so long. She told me that it was okay and not to feel bad, that she would be waiting patiently for me like always and would be no matter what." Mike paused and I stayed quiet offering him ample opportunity to remain composed. His delay was brief then he continued describing his dream at a slow and deliberate pace. "I felt like I needed to reassure her that she was the only one for me, and I had stayed faithful to her not only physically but in my heart. Then I asked her how Chris was doing thinking he was at home with her. Her response confused me in the dream when she said, 'Chris is there with you honey, he's been there with you and could you please give him a big kiss and hug for me.' My dream then skipped ahead and I was on my flight and about to land. I felt all the anticipation I used to feel when I was coming home to see her, and I knew she was there to pick me up. She would always be in the same place, flight after flight, year after year during my playing career. I would get off the plane and see her bright beautiful smile, my beacon in the airport. The dream ended with me walking up the ramp seeing other couples reunited ahead of me just the way it used to be and the tingly feeling I would have right before I would see her again." Mike slumped his head a little, "It really made me miss her, even though it's been over twenty years. That dream took my emotions back in time like it was yesterday." I didn't know exactly how to respond knowing Mike's love and guilt associated with her.

The dream story and his silence prompted me to reflect back on a magazine article I once read on the topic of love and relationships that said statistically a man would fall in love an average of three times during his lifetime. With life experience, I had come to have my own distinctive opinion about such statistics and even though three times may be an accurate average, if every man were being completely honest, he would admit they've only had one love in their life that defined them. The love that would be their crown jewel of loves, the centerpiece of their life with the others unable to completely fill the space left behind in their man's heart or keep it from reaching, even unknowingly for something that could never be touched again if the one true had been lost. I was sure Mike and I had lost ours and all we could do is wait for time to bring her back, that is if being reunited was even possible. I thought about the times I hurt and disappointed my wife with drinking and wished I would have started on the medicine that had been suggested to me by the doctor before I lost her. I wanted her to see I could change. My focus went back to Mike with his head still hung so I veered my constructive thoughts back toward him sending a handful of hopeful, helping words. "I think you're going to see her again Mike and I know she never stopped loving you either."

Mike lifted his chin and sat up straight again then pulled a small piece of paper from his robe pocket. "There's another reason I came to see you," handing me the slip. I immediately recognized the phone number even before I saw the name "Chris" written underneath. "If something happens to me, would you please call him to let him know?" Before answering, I contemplated mentioning my previous telephone call to Chris but couldn't bring myself to confess and even considered making another attempt before something did happen.

"Sure Mike, I'll call him if it comes to that."

"Thanks," Mike replied behind the big brown stache covering his now delicate reserved smile. "You two are going to do fine Tim, as long as you have each other. I guess I should get back to bed before I have some nurse clucking at me like a mother hen." Mike started backing himself up and turned the wheelchair to go back out of our little private area which surprised me considering how weak he appeared earlier.

"Hey Mike, I want to let you know I don't think of you as a baseball player anymore. I think your skills as a human being are far better than anything you did on the pitcher's mound, and I don't know how I can ever repay what you've done for me."

"You can repay me by taking good care of that boy and don't let anything ever come between you." He went back to pushing his wheels forward maneuvering around the edge of the hanging obstacle, and I was under the impression he was putting extra emphasis on our parting and I had to wonder if he knew something more than he was letting on. As he made his way out of my sight, I stood up and gently pulled back the plastic barrier to peak out. Trish was quietly pushing the wheelchair as they were going by the front counter; both of them silent and in the low nighttime lighting, they were soon only shadowy silhouettes disappearing into the darkness toward the elevators. I suddenly and convincingly received the impression Mike had put on a façade of well being and improved strength, wheeling himself around in front of me with Trish hidden in secret, and I couldn't bring myself to guess why. Still tired beyond belief, I tried prohibiting all the stressful things from my thoughts and laid my head back down.

I woke again positioned in the same basic manner as before—in the chair nestled on and against my son. This time though, the motivation to return from sleep wasn't Mike, rather a sliver of sunlight penetrating my eyelids slipping through a small opening in the dark curtains covering the window. Once more, sobering from my exhausted place required a few moments and was a process of awakening back to a clear conscious state. My son looked peaceful resting and I hoped he was doing his crazy twisty dance and joyfully playing in his own prolonged happy dreams. The onset of mild panic could not be repressed as it occurred to me how unhappy and difficult things would be for him if and when he came back into the real world. Were my desires of wanting him back no matter what, selfish? What about severe brain damage, would his waking be subjecting him to a cruel and an unfulfilling life as a vegetable, possibly unable to perform even the most basic tasks. How could I ever take the place of his lost mother and sisters and the confusing pain that would accompany his lack of understanding, defining death for him as they will never come back to see him. My escalating worry slowed some as I conveniently reminded myself that it was all beyond my control, whether or not he woke up and if so if he was completely healthy, either way all I could do is my best. With my welcoming the interjection of calming logic and a new distraction of traveling sunshine, the spiraling fret was unexpectedly rerouted to a check point and at least temporarily detained. The sunlight that had previously crept in as a slender beam in my eye had now morphed into a brilliant white glow against my son's cheek. The mysterious illumination quickly spread over his face then down his body encompassing an area I could no longer logically attribute to the very small opening of the window covering from where it had originated. A flash was the definite momentary peak in brightness causing my eyes to squint then without any ascertainable motive, the glow faded away leaving the room deluded of light as before. As I walked toward the window to peer out in search of a moving dark cloud or a shiny object's odd reflection to somehow begin to explain the strange light that had just surrounded my son, I heard a soft precious utterance behind me, "Daddy."

My heart leaped, "daddy's here," I called out as I hurried to his side. Unsure of what should be done for him upon waking after such a long period, I immediately pressed the button that would retrieve prompt assistance from the medical staff. I took his left hand in mine and leaned over him stroking his head once again giving reassurance that everything was okay, hoping to minimize any fright he may have waking up in such unfamiliar surroundings. Rebecca and another nurse named Crystal appeared almost instantaneously and requested I retreat back a few steps to create needed working space around him. The doctor was then called in and a busy inspection of my child began. I stood helpless at the end of the bed for some time, trying my best to stay in my son's view, "daddy's right here," I softly reiterated several times around their work.

The doctor and nurses asked him their own pertinent questions, performed various tests and checks until finally he muttered, "I'm sleepy."

The doctor, a tall man with clean cut brown hair, who looked about 40'ish and in the prime of his career seemed satisfied with the gotten information so encouraged him to do just that. "Okay, you've been a great help to me, you can go back to sleep now," and my little guy drifted back off.

"Are you sure that's a good idea?" I hastily chimed in, covered in a clear case of head to toe panic, while the relaxed doctor was imparting final instructions to the nurses. The charismatic and composed leader reached out and put his arm around me in a kindly way, a loving lasso to easily escort me to the other side of the curtain where he spoke in a clear but hushed voice.

"As far as I can tell, your son is going to be all right. His body is still trying to rid itself of toxins he inhaled from the smoke. Between the tests, we were able to do while he was unconscious and the cognitive tests I was just able to perform, I'm almost positive he is going to be absolutely fine. Let him sleep, when he wakes up again we can probably get him eating and drinking and maybe even moving around. It may take a few more days nursing him back to health, but all and all, I'm extremely pleased with his progress. Try not to worry Mr. Smith, he'll likely be sleeping for a while again, get yourself some rest or something to eat, we'll keep a close eye on him." The cool and collected physician patted my shoulder and walked off leaving me in a weird emotional place. I was happy he was so sure everything would be all right but terrified my boy might not wake up again and knowing I would have to do the worry waiting game again to find out. I went back into the makeshift room where the two nurses were finishing up with the routine medical maintenance people require when in such a condition. Nurse Crystal extended a smile to me as she departed that closely mimicked the doctor's affirmative expression, and nurse Rebecca followed up with the same but added some greatly needed consolation.

"He is going to be fine, Dr. Romney is one of the best and he wouldn't say it if he wasn't sure." Her words and uplifting smile combined with the others finally convinced me and brought a soothing solace to my aching soul that in turn started a swirling cycle restricted to only relief and coordinated cheer. I would not currently allow the dark area inside me to grow; there would be plenty of time for the oncoming, eventual backlogged grief. This was the only hurdle I could presently handle, saving the others for another day.

"The doctor said he would probably sleep for a while," I stated as a question to the nurse.

"Yeah, considering he just fell back asleep, I imagine he'll be out for a while."

"My friend is down on the fifth floor and I would really like to go tell him the news, but I'm afraid my son might wake up while I'm out. It would only take me about five minutes to run down and back," once more I proposed my question like a statement partly because I hated to ask and split between guilty quickly going and guilty staying knowing Mike would also share in the triumph and could use a slice of positive pie.

"Well here," she promptly pulled a pager from her pocket, "this is for this type scenario. I'll sit here with him and if he wakes up I will page you, how does that sound?"

"That would be great, my friend Mike will love to hear the exciting news," gesturing to my son as I took the pager that would now permit me to deny guilt's shame. "I'll be right back."

I swiftly headed directly to the elevator and down to Mike's floor eager to be the one to report recent events before his supposed undercover spies smuggled in the information ahead of me. Upon exiting the elevator, I could see the door of Mike's room at the end of a long hallway on the left. A crowd was assembled in front of his door that had previously always been open and as I came closer, I could clearly see Dr. Jim, nurse Holts, Trish, Jen, and another man I didn't recognize. Trish saw me approaching and spoke to the group saying something I couldn't make out due to the distance and they all turned to see me coming. A terrible feeling inside me slowed my steps to nearly a drag and I diverted my attention to the walls, uncomfortable with the direct stares. Nurse Holts started in my direction appearing to be on an intercept path. The awful sentiment pushed its way up through my chest and to the bottom of my eyes forcing me to stop walking altogether, finding an island of shelter in the form of a bulletin board hanging halfway between the elevator doors and the assembly of people. I searched up and down the board but couldn't make any sense of it. With my peripheral vision, I could see nurse Holts still approaching and wished she would stop, stop walking toward me, I didn't want to hear what her facial expression couldn't keep from saying.

The words were blurry, I think it's some kind of directory…damn, I don't need directions. I can't read these stupid directions. *How am I supposed to know where to go now?*

CHAPTER 15

I forced a rapid acceptance of Mike's departure in the last few moments before nurse Holts reached me, which began a speedy withdrawal of tears from my eyes with only a final clearing wipe upon her arrival. "I'm sorry Tim." Her simple words conveyed sincere sorrow and not just a redundant line someone in her position may have to use from time to time and exactly what I had come to expect from her. I responded with a pause allowing my last bit of grief to retreat for now, hoping to avoid a woeful word stumble before I was able to share the reason behind my traversing the hallway.

"I only wanted to tell him that my son woke up and they say he's going to be fine. He fell back asleep and the nurse upstairs is sitting with him," I lifted my hand to reveal the electronic hall pass. "She gave me this pager and said she would beep me if he wakes up."

"That's wonderful Tim," her countenance brightened. "Would you mind sharing with the others? They would love to hear about it, we've all been very concerned." I obliged with my cooperative quiet footsteps following hers toward the soft speaking glum group that appeared to be taking Mike's passing harder than I may have thought considering where they work and the short time he was here. As we neared the others, I tried to detour his memory from my mind as preemptive prevention, knowing I may have an embarrassing outburst, a cleansing cry I would rather save for when I'm by myself, next in line right behind the already developing sobbing storm that would soon ravage my emotions…but not now.

We joined the huddle with nurse Holts opening my message, "Tim has some good news." I began slowly and with a nod trying to ease my words into public still bracing for a sad slip, knowing if a slide started I would most likely struggle to recover.

"My boy is going to be fine," and my sentence was halted by an array of elation including a hug from Trish, a pat from the young doctor Jim while Jen executed an almost noiseless but enthusiastic clap-hop movement. After a few seconds I continued, "He's sleeping now that's why I was coming to see—" I stopped there, against my emotional boundary and my kind audience willingly and silently finished the sentence for me. After we all simultaneously glanced down at the floor, nurse Holts gave an introduction.

"Tim this is Chris, Mike's son," she gestured toward the unknown man. I was jolted with surprise he was here and as I reached out to shake his hand, I could now see some of Mike in his features. After my initial shock I remembered it was more his loss than mine so my greeting included.

"I'm sorry about your dad."

"Thank you," his reply startled me again not initially remembering how much he sounded like his dad from our previous phone conversation. He followed our shake with extending an envelope from his left hand. "My dad wanted me to give this to you and I was hoping you may have a minute we could talk.

Nurse Holts spoke again, "Come on gang we all have things to get done." The four dispersed leaving Chris and I alone in front of Mike's door.

Chris pointed to the envelope in my hand, "I think my dad put all my contact information in there before he sealed it." He gave me a half smile rubbing his chin, and I could tell he was giving careful consideration to his upcoming words the way his dad did. "I want to thank you from the bottom of my heart for what you did for my dad and me," his voice remained steady but it was obvious he too was battling the urge to cry. "If it wasn't for your phone call, I wouldn't have seen him before he passed and it was the very best four hours we had ever spent together." Chris paused with a deliberate breath then continued as if needing to cleanse himself. "He got to meet my wife and see his two grandchildren for the first time. You saved him from leaving this world in a terrible tortured state of mind, carrying such painful regrets for so many years. I had no idea how he felt all this time; I was the stubborn selfish one, I should have at least talked to him, I would've known, so thank you again." His eyes now conceded the fight and filled with his own pain and regret and if I hadn't pushed myself to a point of numbness trying to deflect all the sadness swirling around me, I probably would have joined in. I instead consciously and instinctively reached out and two grown men nearly complete strangers simply hugged, and I knew I had found a new dear friend.

After our exchange, Chris shared more details of the past few hours, the happiness and love the two of them were able to share one last time, reunited with their father-son bond. I too knew of this bond that could not be replicated in any other relationship, it was different not necessarily better or more love but unique, like a father-daughter or husband-wife are all different and special in their own way. "Tim, there's another matter I should speak to you about quickly before you go back upstairs. My dad left you some things, things to help you and your son to start a new life." His words once again sprang surprise and along with my heightened emotional state, he had my attention encompassed with laser-like focus. "First, he left you his house."

"His house—" I interrupted his unexpected bomb-shell. "Shouldn't you get his house, you are his family?" I awkwardly concluded. "I wouldn't be comfortable with getting something that should be yours."

"Tim please," Chris calmly chimed in and placed his large hand on my shoulder reminding me again of his dad being large in stature. "We both wanted you to have it, besides I have a nice house that suits my family just fine. He also left you a sizable nest egg."

"Money too, I couldn't accept that, it wouldn't feel right," and self-inflicted guilt smacked the back of my head. "Listen, your dad was my friend. I wanted to spend time with him, I can't take money or a house for that."

Chris exhaled while shaking his head, "He said that you would react this way and in a way it proves his point."

"Point, what point?"

"First of all, my dad knew that you wanted to be here with him and the point is that you are good person Tim, you'll do good things with the money and you'll appreciate and love the house that he loved. He told me if you gave me any trouble to tell you "he was going to hand you the ball in the ninth inning" again, that you didn't let him down before and he knows you won't let him down this time." Chris paused while I tried to absorb and accept Mike and Chris's generosity knowing full well it would make my life easier. He continued while I stayed quiet, "my dad wanted you to have these things Tim and so do I. Besides, I don't think anyone realized how wealthy my dad was. He took the money he made from baseball combined it with thirty-five years of endorsements being one of the most famous people in this city's history and what he didn't give to various charities, he invested very wisely. You're only getting a portion, there's a lot of money going to a lot of different places. I also wanted to mention that my dad confided in me about your depression issues. He did this because I'm a psychiatrist and I'm going to help you with it, I insist." His insisting was in rapid response to my mouth opening, obviously anticipating more of my guilty hesitation.

I finally surrendered, "Thank you, you and your dad are far too good to me."

"Tim, I could never thank you enough." We shook hands again signifying our good-byes and he added, "be sure and call me as soon as possible and we can go over things…and Tim—" I turned back around from my departure in response to his delayed mention of my name, "you're part of our family now." His words sank into my heart and we instantly had the same close rapport his dad and I had quickly blossomed, and my new good friend was starting to feel more like a brother and we both sensed it. I approved of his comment with my smile-nod and was reminded and now felt comfortable enough to ask.

"Chris would you mind if I kept something of your dad's as a memento of our time together?"

"Of course, what would you like?"

"Your dad had a gold and white Bible that an orderly named Henry had given him while he was here, it would be very special for me to have."

Chris went into thought and came back perplexed. "I gathered his things into a box earlier and didn't see a Bible, are you sure he had it here?" Of course, I was sure but where it had gone I wasn't.

I noticed Trish and Jen exiting one of the rooms, a short distance down the hall which put them within earshot of my voice, "ladies." They heard and politely responded to my call by joining Chris and my conversation.

"Did either of you happen to see a gold and white Bible Henry left with Mike the other day?" Trish stayed in character by being the first to answer.

"Henry who?" I briefly considered she was being humorous and I didn't think now was the time but judging by her expression while the two of them waited for my response, I realized I needed to be more specific; there must be many hospital employees.

"You know, Henry the orderly." They looked at each other with a natural inquiry but still produced no recollection leaving me slightly flustered. You guys don't know Henry? He came into Mike's room several times...he knows you." The young nurses recognized my frustrating disbelief and could only apologize when nurse Holts over hearing interjected with her own question.

"Did I hear you say, Henry the orderly?"

"Yes," I said feeling some satisfaction with her apparent knowledge of him.

She followed her first question with, "Was he tall and thin with a mustache?" I nodded then turned toward Trish and Jen with a lip-synched "I told you so," not to be mean spirited but to express I was not crazy. Nurse Holts continued, "Did he have a slight southern accent and a kind warm way about him?" I nodded again and wanted to steer back toward the reason for bringing him up in the first place but nurse Holts stayed strangely compelled to finish her description with questions and as she did we all knew there was going to be a reason for it. "Did he have a lazy eye?" her final question was specific enough, it left no doubt we were talking about the same person.

"Yes, I spoke up this time trying to gain control of the conversation. "Is he around, I could ask him about the Bible he left for Mike we were looking for?" Nurse Holts appeared to be in a deep ocean of thought and not responding. "Nurse Holts, do you know where I can find him?" I repeated.

Her tone came back somber, "He worked here for thirty five years," then without an obvious cause a smile blossomed on her face. We all smiled a smidgen after seeing hers, reflecting relief thinking maybe she had been overwhelmed as of late, producing the peculiar behavior but now was okay.

I followed with the next logical question, "So he's retired?"

"No," she set free a little girlish giggle while wiping moisture from under her eye, "He died...fifteen years ago to be exact."

CHAPTER 16

Upon returning and receiving additional reassurances from the nurse that my son although still sleeping was doing fine, I let myself relax once again back in the chair next to his bed. I was curious as to what the unopened envelope that had originated from Mike and had been given to me by Chris contained but chose the path of wait awhile to find out. My internal psychologist couldn't resist analyzing the two question teeter totter query; was I letting it sit to give myself something to look forward to, or was I afraid the contents could be an emotional salt shaker ready to deliver a stinging pour into a series of fresh wounds. Either way the thought of stalling created a cushion of comfort and with no prodding time pressures in hospital limbo, it wasn't difficult to lay it at the foot of the bed. To continue my new habit of distracting worry and diverting grief, I let my mind wander almost freely only avoiding the one restricted area. I first thought about Henry, "Wow Henry," how cool was that, I got goose bumps. Chris and Mike's reunion and quality time together made me feel good. I was happy for the remarkable loving closure that came at the end for them. My thoughts continued moving forward and I let myself recapture some scenes from Mike and my banter, bonding and honest confiding conversations. I did hope Chris and I would become the same good friends. I never really allowed myself to get too close to people and nothing like a real friend, they took time and I tried to save that for my family...my family, "Damn it," I reached for the letter.

Dear Tim,

There's something I've wanted to share with you, but I've procrastinated to the point now where I thought it would be best to just write it down. I deduced from our previous conversations that you were unaware that I knew your dad. I didn't mention it right away and then I couldn't find the right time but I thought you should know. I didn't realize at first who you were, not until you shared the story of how your father died. Honestly, I don't know why he never told you that we were friends and since I'm assuming you know nothing of our relationship, I thought I would tell you from the beginning. I met your dad at the baseball stadium during the time he worked there as a janitor; you were fairly young and may not remember. Early in my career, I was struggling and nearly out of baseball. One night, I was pitching awful and taken out of the game early. I decided to head into the locker room extremely upset and nervous it might be my last game. Your dad was cleaning at that time and noticed me sitting and pouting in my mitt. I admired the way he approached me, sitting down with the mop in his hand speaking to me like a friend, like he knew me and saying exactly what I needed to hear, and your dad didn't sugarcoat anything. I remember him asking me if I was ready to give up and then telling me some things that I have not forgotten. I believe to this day, these things caused the turning point in my career. I'm not sure if it was what he said, the way he said it, or the timing of the whole thing, but he helped change my attitude and that enabled me to harness my desire to win and focus it on every batter. He started by reminding me what a once-in-a-lifetime opportunity I had pitching in the big leagues, and how many people would do almost anything for the same opportunity. He said, "The next batter will define your career. If he doesn't get hits and get on base, he won't stay in the big leagues and if you don't get batters out, you won't stay. Who wants it more, him or you? Decide every day if you're done playing baseball. If you're not, decide if you're going to let that guy, at the plate, with a bat in his hand take your dream away. I know you have the talent, I've seen you pitch. The next batter Mike, it's always the next batter that decides your fate." Being in sports my whole life, I had heard plenty of motivational speeches but this time it really pissed me off thinking the batter at the plate was trying to steal my dream, and that helped me fight as hard as I could to keep every hitter off my bases. This is where I developed my mean reputation because if someone did get on base, I was coming after him next time. We talked about more things that night but you get the idea. We got to know each other and spoke regularly even after he started a different job. I knew your dad didn't make a lot of money and to show my appreciation from that moment forward, I always left plenty of tickets for him at will call including playoff and World Series tickets. Your dad and I continued to stay in touch even after I retired and would talk on the phone once in a while. That Christmas Eve night, I was there with him at the bar. I had come down a couple hours earlier and we had a few beers together. He said he had to get home by 6:00 p.m., that he had promised you, you could open one present. We said our good-byes, he went out the door and we all heard a commotion. I ran out and he was lying on the ground obviously hit by the car. I put my jacket under his head as he lied on the icy cold sidewalk. While we waited for the ambulance to arrive, he said he didn't think he was going to make it and that he was worried about you and your mother. I told him not to worry I would make sure you were taken care of to ease his mind. Of course, he was right and he passed moments later. After the funeral, I set up a trust fund anonymously for your mother and never spoke about him to anyone again. Your dad was a good friend and you have a good heart like him. I'm very happy we met and I would not trade one minute of the time we spent together. You and your dad have had extraordinary timing and impact in my life. I'm getting tired now I'll finish in the morning.

I slept like a baby and woke up to be surprised by my son. He's walking his wife and kids back out to the car right now. I got to meet all of them what a glorious time we had. I can never thank you enough, he won't tell me what the two of you talked about and said, "It doesn't matter now," he was just happy to be here with me. Well, I'll try and get someone to take this letter up to you and maybe if you have a minute, you could come down and meet him. The two of you would make quite a pair. I know you might have some questions about some of the things I wrote about your dad and I would be happy to answer them. Don't wait too long though, I'm sure time is a luxury I'm running low on.

Your Friend,
Mike

CHAPTER 17

After reading Mike's letter, I felt a tug toward the hurt that had been staying close and impatiently waiting for me to let my guard down again. I didn't want to have another meeting with this bastard, the very reason I have been mightily repressing the thought of my three lost girls, at least not until I got my little guy better and out of this hospital. Then I could think, or cry, or whatever. "I need to keep it together now, be strong for him," I muttered loud enough that I could hear and motivate myself. I can't allow a breakdown but there it was, uninvited and unprovoked, the sinister pain in my heart laughing while welcoming me back to the dark empty place it had previously dragged me off to. I instinctively latched onto an urge to drink, ah yes, my temporary escape. Then thought about Chris and wished I could get some medicine to help me right this instant, some kind of immediate numb, anything that could slow my soul from bleeding out. I bent over as my face fell into my hands, and I could feel a gaping grief hole opening in my chest, filling with tiny slashing spikes laced with defeat, inflicting despair. "Oh God, how am I going to do this alone?"

"You're not alone my boy," answered me and a soothing hand touched my back as I snapped my head up to see...He was sitting next to me in a chair that had not been there before and with his arm now draped around me.

"Henry?"

"Yep, and I am here to tell you that you are definitely not alone." It was strange, knowing what I knew about him now that I wasn't uncomfortable or frightened in the slightest, instead the room was full of a warm, calming...love.

"What do you mean I'm not alone Henry? I sure feel alone. How am I going to take care of him by myself? What am I going to tell him that he can understand about his mother and sisters?"

"Why don't you start with the truth," Henry replied then paused as he sat up straight in the chair. "Tim, they're all fine. Your wife is wonderful and your two daughters are precious."

"You've seen them?" my eyes begged to be loosed. "Please tell me how they are?"

"Tim, they're so very happy. Of course, they do miss you and love you very much, but their only unhappiness right now is due to your unhappiness. They want you to keep on living and have a happy and fulfilling life. You must keep your chin up and not allow the evil in this world to drag you down. Depression can drain you of all hope and that's one thing every person needs; when you lose hope, you lose everything because you have nothing to look forward to except misery. You and your son will need to adapt to a new life, and you'll have each other to lean on. He's stronger than you might think so just be honest and direct with him. Tell him what I told you, that they're doing great, they love the both of you and you'll see them again. The two of you should create new routines and traditions, hang on to your happy memories, but move on. You can never go back and live in the past, although it helped make who you are. The past doesn't have to define you, you always have the freedom to make your own future choices, choose to be happy." Henry paused and leaned forward a little closer. "All your loved ones, family, and friends, they'll all be waiting. You'll see everyone again, I promise. And there's something else I want you to know…God loves you."

I had to turn my head away from Henry to say, "It doesn't feel like he loves me right now or maybe he has favorites and I'm not one of them." Henry's normally pleasant face and happy-go-lucky demeanor quickly transformed, and he now displayed an expression punctuated with a profound sadness that went beyond his face, landing somewhere in a far off place that exists inside all of us but is so distant we barely know it's there. It felt as though he was crying there but without sound or tears. He studied my face for a moment then opened his mouth to speak, but my smoldering anger caused my words to jump ahead of his. "Well, you've been on the other side, tell me what's really the point of all this, why does there have to be children dying in fires? Well—" I stood up to continue the rant with my volume escalating. "Tell me, how all this is supposed to work? Why are we here? How can he love us?" Henry stood up and while facing me placed his two hands on my shoulders and just in time to catch my last gasp, "What am I in this world?" Then without words guided my cheek to his shoulder and he didn't let go… he didn't let go. My clouded eyes soon closed and I drifted off into a light sleep, a dream state where much of my pain dissipated and a few joyful memories played for me. After an unknown period, I lifted my head from Henry's shoulder and quickly returned to an alert consciousness; once there, I was astounded to see three personages standing in front of me. I recognized all three but only after overcoming an initial shock which allowed an opportunity for momentary inspection. Henry was still in front of me, but Mike was to my left and my dad to my right, and all three appeared different. They seemed to be at an age that would have been their physical prime, my guess in their early to mid thirties. All three looked vibrant and healthy with flowing hair, no blemishes, even Henry's eyes were both normal. They were standing amidst a soft glow, wearing majestic white robes that went nearly to their feet that were also adorned with handsome brown sandals. I was stuck in stupefied, and even more surprised when Mike reached out and gave me a big hug that included three solid pats on my back.

Following him, my father reached out and gave me a loving hug, took my face in his hands and said. "I've missed you son," then gently kissed my forehead and added, "It's important for you to listen now."

"Are you ready for me to answer your questions?" Henry asked and I nodded. "Tim, I won't be able to answer every question as fully as you may want, you are not meant to know everything in your current state. We ourselves don't know all the answers to all the questions and mysteries because the learning process continues even for those of us who have already passed. But," he paused for emphasis, "we are meant to evolve and your time here is only a step in that process. Think of your life thus far as the beginning of a long journey; it's a time of testing and opportunity where we learn to differentiate between good and evil, right and wrong." He held his hands up touching his two index fingers together and his two thumbs together to make the shape of a triangle. "Imagine," he started again. "At the top point of this triangle the word 'love', now imagine to the bottom left the word 'serve' and the bottom right 'forgive'. To love, to serve and to forgive one another, these three principals are eternal and the most basic in our learning—they are connected, inseparable."

"You see Tim," Mike started. "When we have genuine feelings of love toward one another, we are more willing to serve others and we all need help from time to time no matter how strong and self-sufficient we believe we are. Needing and giving aid to others is part of God's plan.

"Even the three of us being here right now," Henry spoke again, "is a testament that God loves you and wants to help you through this most difficult time in your life. It's usually through other people he meets our needs and answers our prayers, this is why we serve. This is why it's important to act on promptings and listen to the still small voice when it tells us to do something for someone, the way you did when coming to the hospital to help Mike. By becoming the answer to someone else's prayer, we find answers to our own. Many people believe if they don't assist *this* time, someone else will do the work. Maybe to lessen their guilty conscience after ignoring a prompting, they tell themselves they will do even more next time but that's not how it works. Not following that feeling of service many times leaves the ones needing help without it and the added suffering that follows."

Henry stopped and my dad continued in perfect rhythm. "As we give of ourselves and think of others' needs above our own, we're making a sacrifice; when we sacrifice for others, it enables us to have a deeper capacity for love and a greater ability to forgive. Forgiveness is also something we all are in need of because we all make mistakes, many of which hurt other people. If we hold onto grudges, it poisons our body and corrupts our spirit; if we forgive, it gives others a new chance and we grow spiritually, in ways you can't understand right now, in ways our eternal Father wants us to grow. Just as much as we all need to serve and be served, extend forgiveness and be forgiven, we also all need to feel like we are loved. The feeling of being cared about by others gives us a sense of value. Love is like a light that brightens our way, sunshine that nourishes a plant. Being without love would be like sitting in the dark, alone, and we can't leave our brothers and sisters emotionally unsupported and separated. If everyone lived these three principals to the best of their ability, what a wonderful world it would be. As far as the trials and tribulations we experience, all I can say son so that you can understand is that there is a purpose for everything. Every blade of grass has a purpose, even the slightest breeze across your cheek, and yes, even an awful tragedy has a place."

My father stopped and Mike once again spoke, each taking their turn like a perfectly rehearsed play. "Tim, everyone living has family and friends that have already passed on, people they don't see assisting them in ways they don't know. The three of us being here so that you can see and interact with us is an exception to the rule, but God allowing any of us to help as Henry said shows that he truly loves us all, even you, especially you. You may not feel that way now, but you will, and he does, even beyond our ability to comprehend. There is a method to what some might call madness. What looks like chaos to us is a perfect plan. There is a reason for everything good and bad that happens and not always completely understanding our circumstances is also part of that plan. It's going to be terribly difficult for you but you must have faith, faith that no matter what happens, the Lord loves you and your time of suffering will pass."

He was right and I didn't understand, but I had love and a great respect for each of them and if they said so, I would try. The three men gave me a final hug of assurance and love, and my father explained that they must leave now, but not before Henry gave one last smile and request.

"Would you please give Carol a big hug for me?" I didn't recognize the name.

"I'm sorry I don't know who that is Henry."

His grin inflated, "You may know her as nurse Holts."

"Okay," I agreed but confused as to why I was going to deliver a hug to her from him. And as they began to fade from my sight Henry added.

"Tell her it's from papa," and they were gone.

I sat back down feeling a tiny spark of happiness landing in my own far off place. I knew it would take a lot of work to nurture it into something more but at least I had hope, it was given to me when I needed it most.

My boy began to rustle himself awake and sat up while rubbing his sleepy eyelids. He looked carefully around the room, then surveyed the room again, then at me with his big blue eyes and said, "Daddy, where's momma and sissies?" I held my son.

LOVE

ONE ANOTHER

SERVE   FORGIVE

FROM THE AUTHOR

I hope you enjoyed my book, the characters' sincerity, and the messages sprinkled throughout the pages. If you agree with and hold dear the virtuous ideas I was trying to convey, then please share. Tell people about *Mike Champ*, it does make a difference and let's all be, what we want the world to become. Also by telling others, you're helping the author. This was my first attempt at writing a book and if enough people are interested in this one, it will enable me to write future books. I have many more I would like to write that have Christian themes and what I like to call, "good old-fashioned American values." I miss the America I used to know as a boy; my children will never understand or know her the way many of us remember. God Bless.